GROWING YAMS
IN LONDON

Sophia Acheampong is a British-born Ghanaian. She lives and works in North London and studied at Brunel University. Like Makeeda, she too is still learning about her culture.

GROWING YAMS IN LONDON

Sophia
Acheampong

PICCADILLY PRESS • LONDON

This is dedicated to Mum, Dad, and Gerald.

*Thanks to Brenda, Yasemin, Anne, Melissa and
the rest of the team at Piccadilly Press.
Dr Thomas Mensah for all things Asante
and everything else.
Dr R. Asuboah AKA Nephew and Mr Danso
for the insight into yams and Asante history.
Dr Rose Atfield, Ms E. Aryee, Mrs A Mensah,
Major Elizabeth Osei-Wusu (retired), Mrs Mary Osei,
Mr and Mrs Addai, Mr K. Acheampong for their support.*

First published in Great Britain in 2006
by Piccadilly Press Ltd,
5 Castle Road, London NW1 8PR
www.piccadillypress.co.uk

Text copyright © Sophia Acheampong, 2006

A catalogue record for this book is available from the British Library

ISBN: 1 85340 872 7 (trade paperback)
ISBN-13: 978 1 85340 872 4

1 3 5 7 9 10 8 6 4 2

Printed and bound in Great Britain by Bookmarque Ltd
Cover design and text design by Simon Davis
Cover artwork by Catell Ronca
Typeset by M Rules, London
Set in Lettres Eclatees and Stempel Garamond

Chapter 1

Mel's Party

'Tinted lip-gloss? Check. Mascara? Check.' I spread my make-up out on to the back seat of the car. I caught Dad rolling his eyes at me in the rear-view mirror. He didn't think I should I wear make-up till I was eighteen, but Mum had let me wear mascara and lip-gloss, plus the free sample she got when she bought her favourite perfume. I had to make an effort tonight. It was Mel's fifteenth birthday and she always had guys at her parties, unlike my other friends.

'Don't take any drinks from a boy,' he said, looking at me in the mirror.

'Dad, Auntie Angie and Uncle Kevin will be there,' I said. 'Actually, do you mind dropping me off the road before Mel's?'

I couldn't have him dropping me off at the door. I'd look like a right baby!

'Why, has she moved?'

'Well, no, not exactly . . .'

'Makeeda, are you ashamed of me?'

'No, Dad!'

'The car then?'

'No, Dad,' I replied truthfully.

Dad's a mechanic. He owns a garage in Kingsbury, and we have a great car. I looked up and saw him smirking in the mirror. He was just winding me up.

'Makeeda, I'm not dropping you off on a different road.'

What's the big deal? He's not the one who'll get cold.

'OK then, on her road but not outside her block.'

'Only if I follow you till you get in.'

'Done,' I said.

I was just grateful that Mum wasn't with us. She wouldn't have just taken me to the door. Mum would have gone in with me, picked out potential troublemakers and stayed for a cup of coffee with Mel's parents.

As I walked up the steps to the entrance of Mel's apartment block, I could hear the gentle thud of music. I hoped that my choice of sparkly cranberry top, black corduroy trousers, teal bolero, and dangly earrings looked OK. I pressed the buzzer and saw Mel's stepdad racing down the stairs.

'Hello, Makeeda! You look great.'

It didn't count if your best mate's dad said it, but it was nice to hear.

'Hi, Uncle Kevin!' I said, giving him a hug.

I never called Mel's parents by just their first names, as it's considered disrespectful for Ghanaian kids to do so.

'Is that your dad?'

'Yeah.'

He went outside to chat to Dad and I went upstairs. As soon as I reached the front door, I could hear the sounds of people laughing and a slow song in the background. I gently pushed the door open and saw Mel's cousins, people from our school, and guys from the local boys' school, St Mark's. There were so many people I could barely see the other end of the room. There were lots of thick wires and multicoloured lights beaming across the walls.

'Makeeda!' Mel said, startling me.

She was wearing a gold halter-neck top, a knee-length denim skirt, boots and lots of gold jewellery.

'You look fantastic!' I said.

'Thanks. Dad only let me buy this top if I promised not to wear it out,' Mel said.

I wasn't that surprised. Mel, like all my friends, seemed to be speeding through puberty, leaving me and my flat chest seriously behind.

'Yep, and he's already begged me to change twice,' Mel added, rolling her eyes.

'You're not going to, are you?'

'Hell no! I've already got two phone numbers. It's not bad being fifteen, you know!'

We both laughed.

'Anyway, happy birthday!' I said, giving her a hug and then holding up an envelope.

'Thanks!' Mel said, ripping it open. 'TopShop!' she said, hugging me again, before disappearing.

Great! The only person I can talk to properly, and she's just deserted me. With Bharti at her cousin's engagement party and Nick, my other good friend, spending the weekend at his brother's university, I only really had Mel to talk to till my cousin Tanisha arrived. My mobile beeped so I headed into the kitchen.

Tanisha: There in 10 mins!
Me: Gr8 stuff!

Tanisha's my seventeen-year-old cousin. She used to live with us about five years ago, just after her mum died. Her mum, Auntie Jennifer, was Mum's younger sister. I still remember the day Tanisha came to stay. Her dad, Uncle James, was in tears. He left for a job in America within hours of dropping her off. Tanisha never cried in front of us. Dad told me once that sometimes grief was like that. Tanisha shared my room, so I couldn't escape the weird sobbing sounds she made when she thought everyone was asleep.

After about a year, Tanisha joined Uncle James in America. I hadn't seen her since, but now she'd just arrived in London to stay with us before doing her voluntary work in our grandmother's old village in Ghana.

As I was about to shove my phone away it beeped again.

Bharti: I'm soo bored! Why did my cousin have to have her party this weekend? So, met any gorgeous blokes yet?
Me: Give me a chance!
Bharti: Whatever you do, don't end up fancying the DJ. It's just sad.

Me: There isn't one; Mel's mum didn't want the neigh-
            bours complaining.

Bharti: So you're safe. Gotta go, about to be sprung by an
            auntie. I told her I was catching up on homework I
            missed, but she's discussing it with my mum and
            now I'm getting evil looks.

Bharti had been my friend for what felt like ages. Along with Mel, she was one of my closest mates. She had an older brother, Tejas, and fancied his best mate, Hitesh.

'Could you pass me a glass, please?' said a voice behind me.

'Sure,' I said, clicking my phone shut.

I looked up to see a sweaty guy about my age: tall, dark-skinned, with hazel contacts, wearing a Chicago Bulls vest and looking gorgeous. He was sweating as if we were in the middle of July and not in September. Mel's parents had the heating on, but it wasn't that hot in here. Mel and this guy were the only ones in sleeveless tops; Mel was showing off, but it was her birthday. This guy had no excuse.

'Thanks, I'm really thirsty,' he said.

'Yeah, I can see that,' I said, watching him gulp down the water in seconds. 'I said that out loud, didn't I?' I added.

'Yep!' he said, smiling. 'Are you a friend of Mel's?'

'Yeah, we've been friends since nursery . . .' I began.

'The CD's skipping!' interrupted a guy with red hair and a combination of freckles and acne across his cheeks.

'Damn! Cheers, Stephen,' he said, leaving his glass of water behind. The red-haired guy got himself a drink.

'Excuse me, where's he rushing off to?' I asked.

'He's the DJ, duh!' Stephen replied.

'DJ? But I thought . . .'

'What?'

'Nothing,' I replied, confused. I left the kitchen and headed into the living room as the sounds of the latest number one track flooded the flat. I was immediately whisked to the centre of the room with the other dancers by Mel and her cousins. Within seconds we were all screaming *Free!* along with the track. I noticed the decks in the far corner, with multicoloured stage lights that danced across the room.

'Hey, Makeeda!' Tanisha said, with a slight American accent, as she suddenly appeared in front of me.

'Ohmigod!' I said, hugging her.

'How do I look – English with a dash of American?' she said, pirouetting.

'More like American with a dash of English!'

'Really?'

'Yeah, you look so different,' I replied. That was an understatement. The last time I saw Tanisha, she had braces, thick eyebrows, a flat chest and her hair in cornrows with beads. I stared at her boobs. Either she was wearing a push-up bra, or Uncle James had let her go under the knife.

'I know, I got them done!' she said.

'Seriously?' I said shocked, staring harder.

'These are genetic, sweetie, not cosmetic. I meant my teeth!' Tanisha said, laughing.

'Hey, the DJ keeps looking over here, and I know he's not after me, because I already tried.'

'Really?'

'Oh Makeeda, puhlease? I gotta maaan!' Tanisha said in an exaggerated American accent.

She hadn't completely lost her English accent, so some words came out sounding like a hybrid of both countries. Tanisha showed me a photograph of a guy who looked at least twenty-two.

'Ohmigod!' I gasped. 'He's gorgeous!'

'Hmm . . . I guess so.'

'You guess so?'

'We had a fight before I came over,' Tanisha said.

Her expression reminded me of the look she had when anyone mentioned her mother. It wasn't sad exactly, more a blank look.

'Oh,' I said.

I still hadn't worked out how to break Tanisha's look and I wasn't sure I wanted to.

'Seriously, he keeps looking over at you.'

'No way!' I said.

'Do you think he's cute?'

'Yeah, but he's not interested in me,' I told her.

I only ever attracted weird boys. Never popular ones like the DJ.

'Hmm . . . we'll see. Come on, let's sort out your love life!' Tanisha said, smiling.

'What love life?' I protested as she dragged me towards the DJ. 'Tanisha, what are you doing?' I squeaked, attempting to walk in the opposite direction.

It was too late. We were standing to the side of the decks. The heat was so intense I could feel my make-up melting, so I quickly wiped below my lower lids as my mascara wasn't waterproof. I noticed tiny beads of sweat slowly travelling from the DJ's chin to his chest.

'Makeeda? Makeeda?' Tanisha said, poking me in the ribs.

'What?'

'Ohmigod, just ask him for a song,'

I looked blankly at her.

'Something that I'd like, not that weird stuff you and Nick call a tune. OK?'

If it wasn't rap, hip hop or soul, Tanisha's ears blocked it out.

'Hi,' I said, staring at him. He didn't reply, so I turned to Tanisha. 'Ohmigod, he's ignoring me,' I whispered.

'No he isn't. He's gotta put a track on before he can chat,' Tanisha whispered back.

'So, how am I doing?' he said, shifting his headphone from the ear closest to us. It was lopsided but looked incredibly professional. He was huddled over the decks with an endless number of cables that stretched like huge tentacles around the room. There were records in three piles and a few CDs.

'Um . . .' I hadn't paid much attention to his deck skills.

'What, that bad?' he said, smirking.

Tanisha stepped on my foot.

'Owwreally good! I mean you're really good,' I said, shooting Tanisha a look.

'Thanks,' he said, seeming slightly puzzled as I rubbed my foot.

Tanisha gently prodded me and I stopped. I suddenly realised how totally weird I looked.

'Did you want a song?' he asked.

'Yeah,' I said, as Tanisha left to say hello to an old friend. "Last Kiss"?'

'By 221?' he asked.

I nodded.

'OK, after this one,' he said, smiling. His contacts seemed a little brighter when he smiled.

'Thanks,' I said, hurrying away.

I realised I must have been staring at him. He had a cute smile, but I wasn't telling Tanisha. She was always right. Besides, I'd probably blown it, rubbing my foot and stuff.

'Well?' Tanisha said, grabbing my arm.

'Hey, what did you request?' Mel said, interrupting us.

'"Last Kiss" by 221.'

'Ohmigod, that's a slow song!' Tanisha said in disgust.

I could tell by the look on her face that Mel felt the same way as Tanisha.

'He's good, isn't he?' Tanisha said with a grin.

'Uh huh,' I said.

'He's good looking too,' Mel added.

'I hadn't noticed,' I lied, pulling my eyes away from him.

'Yeah, right!' Mel said, exchanging looks with Tanisha.

'So why did you choose a tune guaranteed to clear the dance floor?' Tanisha asked.

Ohmigod! If no one dances, he'll get a bad reputation and lose work all because I asked for a slow song. Great. I'd totally messed up, and Tanisha was right again!

'Anyway, I thought your parents wouldn't let you have a DJ?' I said, attempting to change the subject.

'I told them that if I didn't have a DJ, they'd end up having to send me to therapy for years because I'd be a Norma No Mates. They chose the cheaper option. Anyway, you should be grateful!'

'Can't believe you chose "Last Kiss",' Tanisha muttered.

'What's the big deal? It's not like I fancy him or anything!' I said angrily.

I stormed off towards the balcony. I hated it when everyone assumed they knew how I felt, better than I did. Mel lived on the top floor of a luxury apartment block that had a balcony with amazing views. I undid the latch and was confronted by a girl with long micro braids, who was kissing a boy with intricate cornrow plaits that criss-crossed his scalp.

'Sorry,' I said, embarrassed.

They reluctantly pulled away from each other, and I received a dirty look from the girl and a grin from the boy, as she dragged him back into the living room.

The door closed and the music became a distant thud.

There were two chairs and a small coffee table surrounded by huge plants. I sat and watched rooms in the flats opposite turn shades of yellow and amber as lights were switched on. A cold breeze swept across the balcony, rustling the plants and sending an icy shiver down my spine. I was freezing.

I heard the door open and felt the music from the living room flow over me, but I stared ahead thinking that Tanisha had probably come to get me.

'Hey! Your cousin asked me to give you this,' said a male voice behind me.

I turned to see the DJ. He was holding a blanket.

'Um, thanks,' I said taking it from him. I was just grateful that he didn't attempt to drape it across my shoulders. That would have definitely qualified as what Bharti calls an RM (romantic moment) or what I call a CM (cheesy moment). I expected him to leave but he took the seat beside me.

'So, how come you're out here?'

I got fed up with everyone saying I fancied you! 'I needed some fresh air,' I said. 'What about you?'

I noticed that he had put a black V-neck sweater on. He must think I'm really stupid coming out here in a flimsy cardigan in the middle of the coldest September on record.

'I . . .' he began, but we were interrupted by another couple kissing and almost falling over us as they burst through the balcony doors.

'Sorry, mate!' the guy said, apologising as they went back into the living room.

'Is this the kissing place or something? That's the second couple I've seen here!' I said.

I really shouldn't have said that out loud. How embarrassing!

'Er . . . I guess so,' he said, staring at me.

I looked away. I'd totally killed the moment. What moment? He can't fancy me?

'So . . . are you taking a break then?'

'Yes, no . . . I mean I've been looking for you,' he said, unsure.

This could be it, undying love declared in September on Mel's balcony. Could this actually be worth freezing my backside off for?

Chapter 2

Mr DJ's break

'I wanted you to request a decent song,' the DJ said.

A song? Request a song? Not declare undying love then.

'Well, I've had enough of playing the usual stuff, especially Fairytale!'

'Hold up. You have Fairytale in your collection?'

I was surprised because Fairytale was one of those pop groups who tried to increase the age of their audience but always failed. Delphina, my little sister, loved them.

'Yeah well, I do kids' parties too,' he said, looking sheepish.

'Ohmigod! You're a closet fan, aren't you?'

'No! Shut up!' he said, pushing me gently.

'Yes, you are! I'm going to tell everyone,' I said, standing up.

He grabbed me around the waist and was just putting his hand over my mouth when we were interrupted.

'Oh er . . . sorry mate, the CD's skipping again and I can't sort it out,' said the red-haired boy I'd met in the kitchen earlier.

'Right, I'd better . . .' he said, releasing me.

'Sure,' I said. Ohmigod, ohmigod that was soo cool, although my lip-gloss was seriously smudged.

'You coming?' he said, just before he went back in.

'Yeah,' I replied, smiling.

As I followed him across the living room, Tanisha pulled me aside.

'So, you got the blanket, but did you get the boy?'

'What are you talking about?' I said, desperately trying to hide my smirk.

'I wanna know everything, Miss I-don't-fancy-him!'

Before I could reply, Mel grabbed us for a dance as the latest Lush track flooded the room. Several songs later, Tanisha and I collapsed on to the couch.

'You don't think he'll think that I don't like him, do you?'

'Huh?' asked Tanisha.

'Well, I didn't go with him to the decks . . .'

'Makeeda, what do you know about DJing?' Tanisha interrupted.

'Nothing.'

'Exactly! Stop stressing and get us some drinks,' Tanisha said, dismissing me.

I wasn't convinced. I headed for the kitchen and on my way back I was stopped in my tracks by seeing the DJ talking to a girl dressed in stretch jeans, three-inch heels and an off-the-shoulder top. Every time she moved her head, her long, blond hair with subtle streaks of vanilla, cream, and honey caught the light like something out of a shampoo ad. She turned and I recognised her. Laura.

'Who's that?' Tanisha said, grabbing the drinks from me.

I could tell she was impressed by Laura's look. Laura always looked at least ten years older than the rest of us. She was never scruffy, her make-up never melted and it was always subtle enough to not be noticed at school by any of the teachers. Laura knew things about being a woman that Mel said her sister Shanice was only just working out. Shanice was twenty-two.

'That's Laura.'

'Why do you look so worried?' Tanisha asked.

'Look at her! She looks great and he's enjoying her company!'

'Oh puhlease! His body language is screaming "push off"!' Tanisha said.

'Who am I kidding? I don't stand a chance if she gets her claws stuck in him.'

'Ohmigod Makeeda, you can't give up already! Haven't you ever heard of a fight? So who is this girl?'

'The one who kissed Nick's exchange student, the French guy everyone knew I fancied.'

'What, Parisian Pierre?'

'Shh! That's what Bharti and I called him. If anyone hears you, I'll never hear the end of it.'

'Sorry. It doesn't mean that Mr DJ is going to ... Don't freak out, but he's staring right at us. Quick, smile he's looking our way,' Tanisha said.

I didn't have time to stretch my features into a smile, but I made an attempt.

'Ohmigod, what was that?' Tanisha asked, hor[.....]
looked like you'd just swallowed a lemon!'

'Shut up! Hi!' I said, as Mr DJ was now standing in [.....]
me.

'Hi.'

'Um, I've gotta . . .' Tanisha said, quickly disappearing.

How obvious was that? I'm going to kill her later.

'So are you taking another break?' I asked.

'Yeah, I think Stephen should be OK on his own for a bit,'
he replied.

'Right,' I said, noticing that the volume had increased
sharply.

I looked at him. He was saying something, but I couldn't
hear him properly.

'What?' I shouted at the top of my voice, just as the track
stopped abruptly. It suddenly felt like millions of eyes were
burning into me. I knew that this moment would be repeated to
everyone at school, and end up being made into an e-mail. Out
of the corner of my eye, I could see Tanisha cowering with
embarrassment for me and Laura giggling with some boys.

Ohmigod, he's definitely going to walk away from me
now! I could barely look at him.

'Do you want another drink?' he said, whispering in my ear.

I nodded. I was stunned and too afraid to speak.

He smiled at me. We went to the kitchen and he poured me
a drink. We stood around kind of smiling at each other and all
I could think was, 'say something, Makeeda!' I heard another
song being played.

'How long have you been DJing?' I asked.

'Um, about six months alone, but I used to help out my cousin.'

'Makeeda!' I spun round to see Mel's mum, Auntie Angie, dressed in a black trouser suit and stilettos. She had long brown hair, immaculately manicured nails, and wore massive hoop earrings. Auntie Angie owned a salon in Harrow, and one in Central London, so she always looked as glamorous as the American models in the adverts for afro hair relaxers. Mel had her looks and, like her mum, was also tiny without her heels.

'Hiya!' I said, kissing her cheek.

'Seeing as you're here, can you help me with this?' she asked.

'Sure,' I said. I held the box as she lifted the cake out.

'Young man, I don't think I'm paying you to chat to my guests.'

'Sorry,' Mr DJ said. 'I haven't played a decent track for a while so . . .' he whispered to me as he left.

'Oh, right,' I said, winking.

Great! I'm stuck in here with Mel's mum and a birthday cake, exactly three walls and a door away from Mr DJ.

But within minutes I was back in the living room with everyone else, waiting for Mel to cut the cake. I was going to find her when she walked in from the balcony, reapplying her lip-gloss, with a sheepish look on her face. It wouldn't have been as bad if there hadn't been a tall boy following her in, from what was now the designated kissing spot. Mel's smirk soon fell off her face when Auntie Angie shot her a harsh look. She cut the cake and Uncle Kevin took some photographs. I later saw him forcing Mel into one of his enormous cardigans in the corridor. Not everyone could see them, but I could. After a minute of attempting to resist him, Mel finally gave up. She rolled the sleeves up and tied it at her waist, but Uncle Kevin made her wear it the way he did.

'Ohmigod, I think Mel's in serious trouble tonight. Did you see the look her mum gave her?' Tanisha said.

'Yep and you won't believe what's happened now,' I said.

'What? Ohmigod!' Tanisha exclaimed, on seeing Mel in the cardigan.

'Makeeda, Tanisha, please sleep over tonight?' Mel pleaded.

'Um, sorry, but Dad's coming to pick us up,' I said, trying not to laugh as she adjusted the cardigan.

'Just call him. Look, here's my phone,' Mel insisted desperately.

'No can do,' I said.

'Nice cardigan, Mel,' Tanisha said, and we both started laughing hysterically.

'He made me put it on! A fantastic halter-neck hidden beneath a bobble-covered, grandad-style cardigan?' she said.

I looked over at Uncle Kevin and realised his former relaxed expression had turned into one of mistrust when any boy came within a metre of Mel.

'I hope you weren't inviting them to stay; we haven't got any more room as your cousins are staying over,' Auntie Angie interrupted, from behind us.

'No Mum,' Mel said sulkily. 'Come on, let's request a song again,' she added, dragging Tanisha and me away from her mother and towards the decks.

'So what do you want to listen to now?' Mr DJ asked me.

'Council Crew's latest?' I asked.

'Thank God!' Tanisha whispered to Mel.

'Sure, I'll put it on after this,' Mr DJ said, smiling at me.

'Thanks,' I said, returning his smile.

'Wait, don't go! Can you find it for me? It should be in that bag,' he said pointing to a black record bag. 'Do you mind picking out two more songs from there, please?'

'I thought that was Stephen's job,' I said, looking through the bag.

'You're better to look at than he is!'

I was gobsmacked. Was he saying that I was good looking? It didn't help that Tanisha and Mel started silently mimicking kisses just out of his line of sight but definitely in mine.

'Um, OK then,' I said.

'Cheers,' he said, as I placed them near him.

'Hey, are you going to dance or what?' Tanisha said, pulling me to the centre of the room, as the intro for Council Crew's latest track began.

We were still dancing three songs later, when one of Mel's cousins told us that Dad was waiting for us downstairs. As Tanisha and I grabbed our coats and said our goodbyes, I noticed Laura walking in from the balcony with Mr DJ. It took me a few minutes to speak. Mel and Tanisha simply followed my eyes.

'Oh great!' I said finally, and turned around.

'No, wait! It's not what you think, Makeeda, look!' Mel said as another boy followed Laura and Mr DJ from the balcony.

'Three is definitely a crowd,' Tanisha added. 'Go and say goodbye to him, then.'

'Happy birthday, Mel!' I said, hugging her. 'He was probably just being nice to me.'

'Makeeda, I don't . . .' Mel replied, but I was halfway out of the room before she finished.

I had a terrible feeling that it didn't mean anything to him. I was feeling too weird about it, so I just continued racing downstairs.

'Ohmigod, Makeeda, what is up with that?' Tanisha said, chasing me.

'What?' I said. There was no way I was going to be shown up by Laura again.

'Why didn't you say goodbye to him?' Tanisha asked.

'Listen, high schools in England may not be as obviously segregated as the ones in America, but there is definitely that thing about cool people like him never looking at people like me . . .'

'Makeeda, you're hardly a geek!' Tanisha interrupted.

'No, but I'm not like Laura or Mel. I know that boys like Mr DJ aren't really interested in girls like me.'

'That's garbage, Makeeda!'

'Hey, why are you two arguing in the cold?' Dad said, interrupting us.

'Uncle!' Tanisha said, hugging Dad.

'I can't believe how much you've grown!' Dad said.

'It's been five years, Dad,' I reminded him.

'I know, Makeeda, but I didn't expect to see a beautiful young lady, instead of the scruffy teenager I knew!' he said, making us laugh.

'Oh, thanks, Uncle,' Tanisha replied.

'You know, you look more and more like Jennifer,' Dad said gently.

I expected Tanisha to go quiet, with that blank expression she got whenever anyone mentioned her mother, but she didn't. I was surprised to see her smiling broadly at Dad's words. She seemed proud.

'How was the party?' Dad asked, as we all got into the car.

'Great!' Tanisha said.

'OK,' I mumbled. My phone beeped.

Nick: How was the party?
Me: Gr8 :(
Nick: Huh?

I was feeling too weird to explain. Besides, Nick wouldn't be interested. All he cared about was maths and smoothies; that's why he did so well in his SATs, was my maths tutor and had sold a load of smoothie recipes to a supermarket. Nick was a year older than me and never let me forget it. We grew up together as our mothers were friends. He reckons we're related, because our maternal grandmothers are from the same village in Ghana and are now neighbours in Kumasi. So, since we were little, he's told people that we're cousins and has always acted that way. That's probably why he switches off when I mention my love life.

I stared out of the window, and left Tanisha to tell Dad how English parties compared to the ones in America. I couldn't shake the feeling that once again Laura had got the one guy I fancied.

Chapter 3

A Bad Hair Day

I looked up at the school gates. It was already four-thirty and most of the other kids were long gone, except for Bharti. Bharti and I had been friends since we met in primary school. We called each other's parents auntie and uncle. She was sitting on the wall reading another horror book, twisting her hair, and holding yet another chewy bar as part of her latest diet. I never saw the point in depriving yourself of your favourite food, but Bharti always had some new idea for losing weight. She was a little bit chubby, but no way as obese as she believed.

'Finally! What took you so long?' Bharti asked.

'I had to help Mrs Hipman set up the Year Seven activities for tomorrow. It's got really cold, hasn't it?' I said, doing up my jacket.

'Tell me about it. Mr Burns kicked me out of the reception ten minutes ago! I thought you had detention?'

'Not exactly,' I lied.

The last thing I wanted was for her to know that I got detention for failing to hand in an essay plan for history. Bharti was always incredibly organised, so couldn't understand why everyone else forgot things like birthdays or essay deadlines.

'She gave me an extension on that history project,' I added.

'Weren't we meant to hand in the essay plans last week?'

'Yeah,' I replied.

'We had ages to find a topic though!'

'I know, but I couldn't find the right one!'

'I suppose it's worth finding the right topic,' Bharti agreed.

'Have you done your science homework yet?' I asked.

Bharti suddenly stopped walking. She crooked her head to the side and gave me a look of disbelief.

'What's up?' I questioned, avoiding her gaze.

'You liar! You weren't helping Mrs Hipman – you had detention!'

'Well . . .'

'Makeeda, you're such a poor liar!' Bharti said, laughing.

'Yeah, I know,' I said, as she caught up with me. 'Where's Mel – netball practice?'

'Nope, it got cancelled, so she's gone to Laura's house.'

'Oh great!' I said sarcastically.

I was annoyed. Mel had barely hung out with us since Laura started at our school.

'It's not like she stole your boyfriend . . . ohmigod, Parisian Pierre!' Bharti said, clutching her mouth as she remembered.

Thoughts of Parisian Pierre floated into my mind. He was gorgeous, sophisticated and French, and had the biggest brown eyes I had ever seen on a boy. He had hung out with Nick and me most of the summer, till Laura moved into the area.

'Makeeda, I'm so sorry,' Bharti added. 'Oh well, you'll always have me as your mate.'

'That doesn't make me feel better,' I replied with a smirk.

'Huh? After I freeze my backside off waiting for you . . .' Bharti said, attempting to whack me over the head with her book as I ducked.

'See, this is what I'm talking about!' I said, laughing.

'You're too rude!'

'I like to see it as being charming.'

'Whatever! You carry on charming people with that mouth of yours, and you won't have any mates left!' Bharti said.

'Cheers.'

'Hey, you never finished telling me about that guy.'

'What guy?' I said, with a blank stare.

'The one you met at Mel's party?'

'How could I forget? I don't know his name, Bharti, but he's gorgeous!' I said. I felt a smile creep across my face.

'Yeah, yeah, like Gary Parks?' Bharti asked, giggling.

'That was a mistake. He tricked me.'

This is why having an old friend can be a problem. Who else would remember that, when I was ten, I got asked out by Gary Parks, a boy I was working on a science project with? When I got to his house, he was dressed really smartly and gave me a rose. It didn't dawn on me what was going on until he gave me a Valentine's Day card and tried to kiss me as we discussed photosynthesis. I hadn't clicked that our meeting was going to take place on Valentine's Day.

'Yeah well, at least I'm not sad enough to fancy my

brother's best mate!' I said, laughing.

'You don't have a brother so . . .' Bharti said, shrugging. 'Hold on, you fancied your mate's brother!'

'What?'

'Nick's brother, Paul?' Bharti said.

'What? That was different!' I said.

I suddenly remembered the day Paul stopped being Nick's mean older brother. Mum had asked me to return their mum's plate, so as usual I jumped out of the car and knocked on their door. Paul opened it whilst drying his hair with a towel. He was almost naked! He did have a pair of jeans on, but I was used to seeing him with a shirt on too. I was so shocked, I nearly dropped the plate. There were muscles and stuff. I couldn't believe it was the same boy who pinched me in the arm, threw mud at my tea party, and nearly ruined Nick's seventh birthday by hiding the cake in a tent in the garden.

'Different how?' Bharti demanded, interrupting my thoughts.

'Well . . .' I began, but I had no idea how to get out of this one.

I stopped when I saw two boys from St Mark's heading our way. They looked familiar, and as they got closer I could see it was Mr DJ and his friend Stephen from Mel's party.

'Ohmigod, Bharti!' I hissed, grabbing her arm. 'That's him!'

Bharti looked at me blankly.

'The one from Mel's party? Mr DJ!' I added.

'Oh right! There are two guys, so which one?' she said.

'The tall, good-looking one, of course!' I hissed at her. Bharti never really listened to me.

'Ooh I'm glad you said that. The other guy really isn't your

24

type. I've seen less spots on a Dalmatian . . .'

'Bharti!'

'Sorry, but he has. I don't know if I can even look at him,' she continued.

I gave her my 'don't go there' look.

'What?'

'Well, remember when you had that allergic reaction? You were covered in spots and didn't want to leave the house,' I said.

'Yeah, but that was different.'

'Please, I'm begging you, don't mess this up for me. I have enough trouble being myself around this guy, without you being all weird with his mate,' I said.

'I wouldn't do that!' Bharti replied indignantly.

'I didn't mean . . .' I began, but I stopped when I realised they were less than ten metres away from us. 'Ohmigod, they're about to walk past us. I can't find my lip-gloss!' I said, frantically searching my bag. 'Oh maaan!'

'Here use mine,' Bharti said, handing over hers.

I quickly turned away from them and applied it, whilst tugging my hair free of its band. I knew I owed her an apology, but I still thought that she was being mean about Stephen's spots.

'All right?' said Mr DJ.

'Hiya,' Bharti said, smiling.

I snapped my head round and nearly blinded him with a stray braid.

'Ohmigod!' I said. 'Are you OK?'

'Um . . . yeah, I think,' he said, clutching his eye.

I looked over at Bharti who was trying desperately not to burst into laughter. I shot her a look.

'I'm so sorry!' I was devastated. I'd already lost any chance of going out with this guy.

'Braids sometimes have a mind of their own,' Bharti said.

That caused the biggest grin to come on to his face. I flashed a smile at Bharti.

'I'm fine. My sister's hair does the same ,' he said, grinning.

At that moment I couldn't have loved Bharti more.

He wasn't much taller than me, but he towered over his friend. He had a black polo neck on under his school shirt and his hazel contacts looked almost natural against his ebony skin tone.

'They should come with a health warning . . .' I added.

'Hey aren't you Tejas's sister?' asked Stephen.

'Yeah,' Bharti replied hesitantly.

'I thought so! What's your name?' he asked.

'Bharti.'

'I'm Stephen.'

That was the only part of their conversation I caught, as Mr DJ began talking to me. I stared at him, too stunned to listen properly.

'Makeeda?' Bharti said, raising her eyebrows at me.

'Yeah?' I said, coming out of my daze.

'She's only just changed networks,' Bharti said and rattled out my mobile number.

'OK, I'll text you about the party then?' Mr DJ said to me.

'Sure,' I said, watching him and Stephen walk away.

I knew there was no way my parents would let me go to a party if they'd never met the person holding it. I was just pleased he had my number.

'Bye, then,' he said, turning to smile at both of us.

'When did he mention a party?' I hissed at Bharti. 'Wouldn't mind going if he was there though,' I said dreamily.

'Oh boy, you've got it bad!' Bharti said with a grin.

'What do you mean?'

'Ohmigod, your hair! What was that all about?' Bharti was almost shaking with laughter.

'I know. Talk about embarrassing!' I said, laughing too. 'Thanks for . . .'

'Yeah, yeah. Anyway, what's his name again, Makeeda?'

I looked blankly at Bharti. I didn't remember giving him mine either. This was a disaster! I was so glad Bharti had been with me.

'I'll tell you his name if you buy me a nice, expensive hot chocolate,' Bharti said giggling.

'Deal,' I said. 'Bharti?'

'Yeah?'

'Thanks for not making me look a complete idiot,' I said and I hugged her.

'Well, it's not easy, but when you've got a job to do . . .'

'Hey!' I said, whacking her across the head.

'That's it, I'm going home!' Bharti said jokingly. 'You hit me!'

'What? Come on, Bharti, please? You haven't told me his name yet . . .'

'Blimey, you really do have it bad! Beg some more and I'll think about it,' she said, rushing down the road as I began chasing her.

I didn't want to say it out loud, but she was right. I did have it bad. My biggest problem was working out how to see him again.

Chapter 4

The Bookworm Wannabe

I stared at the stairs ahead of me. It was four-fifteen and I had a maths lesson with Nick at five p.m., so I had forty-five minutes to sort out my history project. The threat of a letter being sent to my parents was no way for anyone to live. I was beginning to get stressed out. For some reason, I didn't want to just hand in an essay plan based on the first female biography I found in the library. Mrs Hipman said we had to find an inspirational individual. It would be easy enough to just write a paragraph at the end saying why I chose this woman, but I actually wanted to mean it when I said this person inspired me.

I climbed the stairs to the public library and was surprised by the number of posters for Black History Month. I walked in and saw more posters and a display of African artefacts alongside a piece of ntoma cloth that was acting as a backdrop to books written by mainly African American authors along-side novels by Black and Asian British writers and biographies of Black and Asian footballers and actors.

As I flicked through a book about the Transatlantic Slave Trade, I began to wonder if Aunt Grace was right. She said Black History Month was like Carnival: the one part of the year when it was cool to be Black. Mum said that Aunt Grace could be bitter at times, and that things were no longer as bad as twenty or thirty years ago. When I asked her what she meant, she told me how they used to cheer when a black person was on television, then how that changed to hoping that the black actor in the detective programme wasn't playing a criminal, as usual. I was really shocked as I thought actors got to play different parts regardless of their race. At school no one ever made a big deal about stuff like that and we've always had multicultural performances, although in nursery Auntie Angie had to come in when Mel was told she couldn't play Gretel in *Hansel and Gretel* because she didn't look like the girl in the book.

I found a desk and dumped my coat and bag on it. I headed for the history section but got bored looking for the perfect material, so I returned to my desk and flicked through a book on the Crimean War. I was about to make notes on Mary Seacole for my history project, when my phone rang.

'Switch it off!' screamed a librarian, as I ran out of the library.

'Hello?' I gasped.

'It's me!' Mel said. 'Why are you out of breath?'

'I've been running.'

'That's why you should be on a school team, with Laura and me.'

'Mel!'

'Seriously, after a month of training you'd be so much fitter!'

Great, I had Mel going on about my lack of exercise and Laura agreeing in the background.

'Mel, I'm freezing my butt here, what's up?' I asked, irritated.

'I needed to know if you wanted to come bowling tonight.'

'I can't. Mum would kill me if I went out on a week night.'

'Ahh maaan! Makeeda, you don't have to tell her everything, you know!' Mel said, sighing. 'I'm about to hand that DJ to you on a plate!'

'Seriously, Mel, I can't, not even for Nelson.' Bharti had told me his name after two low fat hot chocolates. They were expensive but worth it.

I hadn't told Mel that he had already sent me a text. He said he was just checking he had the right number, but it was a start.

'Laura thinks you're mad to give up on seeing that guy.'

I wanted to scream that I hadn't given up on anything, but I didn't want Laura knowing my business.

'Look, I'd better go,' I said.

'Where are you anyway?'

'The library.'

'B-O-R-I-N-G!' Mel intoned.

I could hear Laura giggling in the background.

'Whatever!' I said, cutting her off.

Sometimes Mel was mean. She had probably already done

her homework, but I still had Mrs Hipman's project, on top of everything else. I stormed back into the library and fished out a magazine from my bag. Mum hates me reading too many magazines, so I hide them. Gradually I began to calm down, especially when I saw an article on ten ways to tell if a boy fancies you.

Step one: Does he ignore you or pick fights with you? Hmm . . . Nelson did pick a fight at Mel's party, when I said he liked Fairytale.

Step two: Does he hit you playfully? This is a boy's way of achieving physical contact. Yes, he definitely did that when I . . .

'Ouch!' I said, looking up to see Nick.

'All right?' he said and slid into the seat opposite me.

Nick is tall and skinny (despite his ability to eat more joloff rice and fried plantain than anyone I'd ever met). His mum is Ghanaian and his dad is Polish, so Nick has brown ringlets he wears like a mop, Caucasian skin and green eyes. Mel thinks he is fit but all I see is the boy who threw up on me when I was eight, and gave me chickenpox when I was ten. The only time I've ever been grateful to have him as a family member was when José Santos bullied me in primary school. Nick was in the year above me, and that was a year below José. Despite this and his skinny little frame, when Nick saw me being pushed around in the playground during lunch break, he pushed José so hard that he fell backwards and ended up with a sprained wrist. When the teachers arrived, José was too embarrassed and in too much pain to tell them Nick had pushed him. Since then, the legend that is Nick's strength has meant that no one has even breathed too hard in his direction. He never talks about it. Even now when I tease him, he just changes the subject.

'Do you mind?' I said, rubbing my head.

This was his usual way of saying hello: I get whacked across the head with his latest reading book, and he just smirks at my discomfort.

'No,' he said, pulling one of my braids loose.

'Keep the noise down,' said a library assistant, shelving books to our left.

'Ohmigod, how many times? Don't. Touch. The hair!' I said angrily.

'Whatever. Shall we start?' he said, removing the scariest looking maths text book from his bag.

'Er . . . we're not using that are we?'

'Makeeda, you can barely add. Why would I use an AS-level book to teach you? It's for me to use while you're doing some of the exercises in here,' he said and took a smaller GCSE textbook from his bag.

'I knew that! I was just mucking around,' I lied.

Nick already thinks I'm dumb: I don't want to give him any ammunition.

'Yeah?' He had a smirk on his face.

I really wanted to know his opinion about Nelson, but Nick and I never really spoke about relationships. He even looked embarrassed when I bumped into him and his ex-girlfriend Maria last month. They weren't kissing, but he went the shade of a bus (well, a red one) and all I said was hi.

'Can I ask you a question?' I said.

'Seriously, Makeeda, we have to get on with the lesson. I've got revision to do after this. You do know this is my GCSE year?'

'Yeah.'

'If I fail, I'll have to do retakes and my first choice for sixth form goes out of the window . . .'

'Nick, you're not going to fail! You're already way beyond GCSE level.'

'If you two don't keep the noise down . . .' began the librarian.

'Sorry,' we chorused.

'OK, but in here it says that if a boy likes you . . .' I began in a whisper.

'Give me that!' he said, snatching the magazine from me. 'Makeeda, you're meant to work this out for yourself!'

'I . . .'

'It's simple. Just add up the points to see which one of the four sad categories your love life falls into.'

I switched off at that point. I wasn't sure what was worse. The fact that I had just confirmed how thick I was, or that Nick was enjoying making me look that way.

'Makeeda?'

'I know, I know. Sad.'

'Yep and it's stupid, so can we just get on with the lesson?'

'Fine. Here are the exercises from last week,' I said, handing over my work for him to mark.

'Great. We're doing quadratic equations today.'

'But I don't need to know that till next year!' I protested.

It's one thing to force me to have lessons, but when he starts messing with the topics on my syllabus I get annoyed.

'Makeeda, that's the point. I'm tutoring you for your GCSEs? Duh?'

I decided there was no point in arguing.

Over the next forty-five minutes Nick taught quadratic equations as well as Pythagoras' theorem. Just as I was finishing off some exercises, my mobile phone beeped with a text message from Nelson.

Nelson: All right? W R U?

'Makeeda, this is a lesson?' Nick said, annoyed.

'Hmm,' I said, mesmerised by my phone.

Ohmigod, what do I say? I mean, if I tell Nelson I have a tutor then he'll think I'm thick, but if I tell him I'm at the library he'll think that I'm a geek.

'Hello, anyone in there?' Nick said finger-flicking my forehead.

'Ouch, what was that for?'

'Maths lesson – ring any bells?'

'What?'

'Who is it?'

'No one,' I said, attempting to put my phone away.

I was too slow; he grabbed the phone.

'Who's this?'

'Er . . . a guy from Mel's party.' I wasn't sure how much to tell Nick. It was too embarrassing.

'Oh, a guy you fancy from Mel's party.' He smirked.

'Yeah, yeah. OK, so I like him.'

'So what are you going to say?'

'I dunno. What do you think?'

'You could tell him the truth, but then he might think you're a geek, or really thick.'

'I know.'

'Or say that you're somewhere else?'

'Brilliant!' I replied, and typed my reply.

Me: I'm out with my parents.

'Ah huh! Lying to a partner. Isn't that some kind of major issue in your magazines?'

Ohmigod. I've just lied to the guy I want to go out with. This makes us candidates for every daytime chat show, before we've even gone on our first date!

'Makeeda? Makeeda, I'm just messing about. Are you OK?' Nick said, worried.

'Yeah, I'm fine!' I realised I must have had an odd look on my face or was breathing erratically.

'You're not going to cry or anything? I would've sent the same text message as you,' Nick said.

Nick hated to see me cry. Tears just seemed to embarrass him. I stared at him and saw his face getting redder with concern for me.

'Listen, let's finish up. You don't have to do all that page as homework, just the first two questions,' he said.

I guess he wasn't that concerned after all.

'Do you want me to walk you home?'

'Er no, why?'

'Don't look at me like that! I thought . . . never mind, just text me when you get in.'

'Yes, Uncle Nick,' I sang back.

'Shut up, it's dark and stuff out there,' he replied, hastily packing up.

'Bye.'

'Yeah, see ya,' he said and walked away.

A minute later I looked up and he was watching me from the double doors.

'What?' I silently mouthed, but he just waved goodbye.

Nick was like the older brother I didn't want, or need. I began to pack up my things when my phone beeped again.

Bharti: I hope you've started that history project!

Ohmigod, I completely forgot!

Me: No worries I'm in the library.
Bharti: U 4got didn't u?
Me: I wouldn't say that exactly. Chat later. x

I unpacked my things again and headed back to the history section again. I had to find someone I found inspiring. A woman who fought against the odds like Mary Seacole but wasn't Mary Seacole – everyone seemed to write about her. I wanted to find the right heroine and the more I thought about it, there was no reason she couldn't be Ghanaian or at least African, was there?

Chapter 5

Tanisha's Experiment

I opened the front door, threw my bag against the wall, hooked my coat in the cupboard and slipped off my school shoes. I heard laughter coming from the kitchen and noticed Tanisha's red coat on the next hook.

'Makeeda?'

'Yes, Mum?' I said, walking into the kitchen.

Mum was peeling a huge piece of yam, so I planted a kiss on her cheek. Tanisha was stirring some garden egg stew.

'Good, you're back. Did you get much research done?' Mum asked.

'Sort of,' I lied.

I'd spent yet another evening at the library and found nothing. My parents thought I'd already started my history project and believed the extension was my real deadline.

'Hey!' Tanisha said, hugging me.

'All right?' I smiled back, but I wasn't being genuine.

I hated seeing them together. It didn't help that Tanisha has the same features as Mum, except she is bigger like her own mum was, and tall like Uncle James. Even Delphina and I don't look like Mum.

'Dinner will be a while, so why don't you get some homework out of the way first?'

'Yeah, OK,' I replied reluctantly, and headed out of the kitchen.

I didn't want to leave them. They always seemed to have fun together in a way that excluded everyone else. It had always been like that.

'I hope you haven't left your bag by the front door again?' Mum called after me.

'No,' I said, retrieving my bag.

I used to just leave my bag and carry the books up to my room, but Dad sprained his ankle a few months ago, tripping over it as he walked into the house. I got into loads of trouble, but no one remembered that he'd been tipsy anyway.

Delphina popped her head round the corner from the living room.

'I'm telling Mum,' she said, shaking her braids at me for emphasis.

Delphina looks like Dad and is fair, whereas I am dark like Aunt Grace and look like her dad, my grandfather. Delphina's first words weren't 'mama' or 'papa', they were 'I'm telling' and nothing much has changed in nearly ten years.

'Not if you want help with your art project,' I said.

'Deal,' she said and disappeared again.

I grabbed my bag and headed to my room. I read my English textbook and answered some questions for RE and helped Delphina. An hour later, I was finishing off my answer to question two of Nick's maths homework, when Tanisha popped her head round the door.

'Dinner's ready, Makeeda.'

'Thanks.'

I walked downstairs and found Aunt Grace already seated at the table along with Delphina and Dad. Aunt Grace usually had dinner with us before doing a nightshift, as our house is closer to the hospital than hers.

'Go and give them a hand,' Dad said.

'OK,' I said, heading to the kitchen.

I only got as far as the doorway when I stopped. Mum was watching Tanisha transfer the stew from the saucepan to a bowl, with the biggest smile on her face. It all came flooding back from five years ago. Tanisha and Mum going to the shops, with me feeling like a spare part, clinging to Delphina for company, and the time Mum took nearly a week off work simply to hang out with her niece. It was like Delphina and I didn't exist.

I'm so selfish! Tanisha had just lost her mum, Mum's sister, she needed a mum. I guess she will always need mine.

'Makeeda?'

'Huh?' I said, snapping out of my thoughts.

'Take those plates in, or they'll only be able to stare at the food Tanisha's just put out,' Mum said, smiling.

'Yeah,' I replied, but I couldn't return her smile.

We sat around the dinning table and, as everyone closed their eyes in prayer (something that was only ever done at Christmas, Easter and when Aunt Grace was with us) I looked around the table. Delphina had her eyes scrunched up in concentration, and was sitting between Dad and Aunt Grace. Mum was sitting next to Tanisha, as usual. As we ate, the conversation focused on Tanisha's inability to choose between going to a British or American university. Mum was eager for her to choose one in Britain. I wasn't so sure. I'd miss her if she was in America, but I knew that if she was here, I'd have to deal with the whole Mum and Tanisha thing again.

After dinner I went to my room and a minute later Aunt Grace was at my door.

'Why were you so quiet at dinner?' Aunt Grace asked.

'No reason,' I replied.

I couldn't tell her the truth. Aunt Grace was the last person in the world I wanted to annoy, and I knew she'd just think I was being selfish about Tanisha and Mum.

'It's nice having Tanisha around, isn't it?'

'Yes, it is,' I said, hoping she hadn't noticed the strain in my voice.

'Tanisha's lucky to have your mum around.'

'Uh huh,' I said and averted my eyes.

'But really lucky to have an understanding cousin like you.'

Ohmigod, she knows!

'Auntie, what do you mean?' I asked, looking up.

'Makeeda, I know that it's difficult for you.'

'Uh huh,' I said.

'Do you feel jealous?'

'Uh huh.' To my horror tears started rolling down my cheeks. I'm not a baby, but I always felt like one when it came to Mum and Tanisha. 'I don't mean to be, Auntie, it's just so . . . so unfair!' I blurted out.

'It's OK, Makeeda,' she said, hugging me. 'I know you're not a bad girl. You're just a good girl caught up in a difficult situation. Now stop crying; go and wash your face.'

I did as I was told and overheard Mum and Tanisha's laughter from below.

'It will get easier,' Aunt Grace said with a smile, on my return.

'When, Auntie?' I asked, but she pretended not to hear me and handed me a plastic bag.

'Here you go. This might cheer you up.'

'Thanks. Oh, it's *Agoo Magazine*!' I said, immediately leafing through the glossy pages of West African socialites, photographed in the style of *Hello* magazine.

'On page forty-two is the woman you met at my house last month.'

'Which one?' I asked, hunting down the page. I'd met four women at Aunt Grace's house when they'd all gone round to buy some ntoma from her.

'You know, the one whose daughter's on that TV programme in America.'

I still had no idea.

'Do you remember the woman with a bright yellow scarf?'

How could I forget? I remember being accosted in the corridor at Aunt Grace's place by a woman in her sixties wearing a red winter jacket, blue hat and bright yellow scarf.

'The one with the really bad weave?'

'Makeeda!' Aunt Grace said, trying to suppress a smile.

'Ohmigod, that's her?' I studied the photograph of the same woman dressed in a yellow, green and red Kente. She had her hair swept up in a bun and make-up that made her look like a celebrity. 'Wow! So she changed her hairdresser then,' I added.

'Makeeda, stop that!' Aunt Grace said, laughing. 'Right, I'm off. Make sure you finish your homework before you start reading that. I know your mum prefers you to read it at the weekend – this was a one off. Therapeutic.'

'Yes, Auntie,' I replied closing the magazine and tossing it aside.

I hugged her and watched as she closed my bedroom door. I was sure this was her way of taking my mind off Tanisha and Mum. I waited two minutes to hear her feet on the stairs.

'All mine now!' I said, diving onto my bed with the magazine.

'Ah ha! I've caught you!' Aunt Grace said as she burst back through my door. 'I knew you couldn't leave that thing alone!' she said, smirking.

'I was just reading an article for my homework,' I lied.

I scanned the contents page and found an article on Yaa Asantewaa, who was the Queen Mother of Egweso in the late 1800s.

'Which one?' Aunt Grace asked.

'Yaa Asantewaa,' I mumbled. Please let that be right.

'Oh good! Then I'll leave you alone,' Aunt Grace said, leaving my room for a second time.

I'd better read it in case she tests me later, I thought.

In 1900 Yaa Asantewaa, the formidable Egweso Queen Mother, engaged the British in one of the last wars involving the Asante Military.

Hey, maybe I really could use this for my project! At last, a legitimate reason for Mum to not hide the magazine from me! Mrs Hipman's going to be so impressed!

My mobile beeped.

Nelson: Wot u up 2?
Me: Homework :(
Nelson: Just finished mine :)
Me: Stop showing off! ;)

Why hasn't he replied? Ohmigod, what if I didn't put the wink at the end of the sentence?

I quickly checked my sent messages and breathed a sigh of relief: it was there, but Nelson still hadn't sent another message. I checked the time he sent his last message: it was 8.16 p.m. and I'd sent mine at 8.19 p.m. I looked at my watch; it said 8.30 p.m.!

I threw myself onto my bed and screamed into my pillow. Why was Nelson taking so long to reply?

My phone beeped again.

Nelson: Do you want to come out on Sunday? I can't do Saturdays in term time.

I stared at the message. Then I screamed and started dancing around my room.

Tanisha rushed in. 'Makeeda, are you OK? Your dad asked me to —'

'Tanisha, you're not going to believe this! Look!' I said, shoving my phone in her face.

She screamed. 'Ohmigod!'

'I know, I know!' I said.

'What is going on in here?' Dad said angrily, appearing in my doorway.

'Nothing,' Tanisha and I chorused.

'Then why are you both screaming?'

'Sorry, Dad,' I replied.

'Right, well, stop that nonsense. Delphina's trying to sleep,' he said.

'Sure, Uncle,' Tanisha said.

As soon as Dad left, Tanisha grabbed me by the shoulders. 'Makeeda?'

'Yeah?' I replied, dreamily staring at my phone.

'I hate to point this out to you, but you haven't replied.'

Tanisha covered my mouth before I could scream loudly.

'Ohmigod, do you want your parents to know or something?'

I couldn't see why not. I mean I lie to them about the small stuff but never anything this big. I couldn't think about that now, I had to reply to Nelson.

Me: OK. What time?
Nelson: 5pm?

Me: OK, Where?

Nelson: My dad will be out so you can come round.

'Well?' Tanisha asked impatiently.

   'He wants me to go to his place.'

   'For a first date? I don't know, Makeeda. I'm sure that like breaks soo many dating rules!'

   'In the States maybe, but . . .'

   'I'm serious. He could do anything to you . . .'

   'Ohmigod, Tanisha, stop it!' I said.

   I knew she had a point, but I didn't think Nelson was like that.

   'Call me every hour,' Tanisha said.

   'What?'

   'If you're going to his place, then I want to know you're safe. Better still, I'll teach you some defensive moves,' Tanisha said.

   Tanisha had taken self-defence classes in the USA, and had already taught her favourite moves to Mum and basically any other woman she came into contact with. So far, I'd managed to avoid it, but I knew she wasn't going to let me get out of it now.

   'You know, my parents won't mind . . .' I began.

   I was interrupted by Tanisha laughing hysterically.

   'Girl, sometimes you're so funny!' she said, clutching her stomach and doubling over.

   I wasn't laughing.

   'What now?' I said, folding my arms across my chest to stop me hitting her. I hated it when she did her all-knowing older cousin thing. I always ended up looking stupid.

'You can't tell your parents,' she said.

'Why not?' I asked.

'There is no way they'd let you go,' she said in a matter-of-fact tone.

'They might,' I replied, irritated.

Just because she was older, it didn't mean that she knew everything. Mum and Dad wouldn't have that much of a problem with me having a boyfriend. I am fourteen, after all. Besides, Mel's had a boyfriend since she was twelve and her dad can be as strict as mine.

'OK, I'll prove it to you. Follow me,' Tanisha said.

We headed downstairs to find Mum curled up on the sofa flicking channels, and Dad sitting at the dining table engrossed in a Haynes car manual. Tanisha sat next to Mum, whilst I sat opposite Dad at the dining table.

'That's a good show, Auntie, you'll like it,' Tanisha said.

'Thanks, what's it about?'

'Well, you see that woman on the right? She's a detective and struggles with the whole work–life balance thing.'

'Hmm . . .' Mum replied.

'Yeah, and she has this teenage daughter who she caught dating a boy, like, three grades above her,' Tanisha added.

'Oh dear.'

'Then she messed up on a case and nearly lost her job.'

I couldn't really see where this was going, so I caught Tanisha's eye and tapped my watch. I still had to reply to Nelson and her experiment was taking for ever.

'Auntie, how old were you, when you had your first boyfriend?'

'Well . . . um, I was about twenty.'

Dad coughed like he was choking, then disappeared behind his manual.

'Need some water?' Mum asked him.

'No thanks,' Dad mumbled.

'Twenty?' I said, shocked.

'Really?' Tanisha added.

'Yes. Personally I'm glad. I don't think it is right for young girls to have boyfriends at an early age.'

Ohmigod! Tanisha's right.

'So how old do you think is right?' Tanisha asked.

'Well, at least eighteen.'

That's it, my life is over! How can I tell Nelson to wait four years before going out with me? Why, why did my mother have to be a late bloomer? This is so unfair!

'You see at that age you're practically an adult . . .' Mum began.

'Um, aren't you legally an adult at eighteen in the UK?' Tanisha asked.

Ohmigod, I can't believe Tanisha said that. Is she crazy? Mum is so going to spell it out.

'Yes, but not in this house,' Mum replied sternly. She held Tanisha's gaze in the process.

'I see. Well . . . it's good to know,' Tanisha said, averting her eyes. I could tell she was embarrassed.

'Tanisha! Can you help me with something on my computer?' I said, jumping from my seat. Dad looked at me curiously.

'Sure, Makeeda,' she said, smiling brightly.

We got to my room before I spoke again.

'Thanks for that, but—' I began.

'Listen, if you want to see him, you have to lie,' Tanisha interrupted.

'Seriously?'

'Yeah, unless you actually want to wait till you're eighteen?'

'Ohmigod! I hate this,' I said, reaching for my phone.

I knew she was right though. There was no point telling my parents. They would never let me meet him.

Me: That's fine. Text me your address.

Nelson: U took ages! I thought u'd turn me down.

Me: Nah just had 2 sort something out.

Nelson: Get the bus 114 and get off a stop before Kenton station. I'll be at the bus stop.

Me: OK. Nite.

Nelson: Nite.

'Are you going to be around on Sunday?' I asked Tanisha.

'Nope. I'm staying with Auntie Mary. You know, my mum's friend from uni.'

'Oh yeah. Damn! I can't use you as an excuse then.'

'Bharti.'

'Bharti?'

'Yeah, all you have to do is show up at Bharti's, stay for a few hours, and then go to Nelson's,' Tanisha said.

'That's risky. I mean at Bharti's – I could end up staying longer.'

'OK then, just pretend you're going to Bharti's . . .' Tanisha said, just as the door opened.

'Tanisha, your Auntie wants you,' Dad said interrupting us.

'OK,' Tanisha replied.

'Makeeda, are you all right? You look worried,' Dad said.

'Oh it's nothing. Dad, um . . . is it OK for me to go to Bharti's house on Sunday?'

'Yes, of course it is,' Dad replied. 'Is that what's been worrying you?'

Blimey I can't lie again, can I?

'Well, sort of . . .' I said.

'You really are a strange girl sometimes!' Dad said, flicking my braids before leaving my room.

I gave him a huge grin as I grabbed my phone to tell Bharti.

Tanisha better be right about all of this lying or I'm a dead girl.

Chapter 6

Nelson and Stuff

Bharti picked Monday of all days to be ill. That left me with no one at school to talk to about my date. Mel was totally preoccupied with practising for the latest netball try-outs during every break we had. Plus, because of Tanisha's weird 'trust no one' rule, I had texted her every hour just to let her know I was safe, so she'd already got my date details on Sunday night.

My phone rang as I walked home.

'Hello?'

'It's me. When are you going to get home?' Bharti asked.

'Calm down. I'm two doors away.'

'Calm down? You tell me via text you had a "nice" time and leave it at that? Girl, that was over twelve hours ago! I want details, so hurry up!'

'Well, if you'd been in school . . .' I said as I opened my front door.

'Shut up and get on MSN!' said Bharti, ending the call.

Talk about rude! She can wait till I've had a bit of tea and toast, I thought. I headed for the kitchen. Within ten minutes the house phone rang.

'Have you even switched on your PC?'

'Well . . .'

'Ohmigod, you made tea and toast, didn't you?' Bharti said in an accusing tone.

'Well . . .' I said, taking a bite of warm toast coated in melted butter and strawberry jam. I couldn't help it. It was like a ritual: get home, make some tea and toast.

'Makeeda, you know if my parents catch me on the phone they'll kill me and make it look like an accident!' Bharti screamed.

'Yeah, yeah, sorry – two minutes tops!' I told her.

During the summer, Bharti had managed to hike up her family's phone bill by nearly a hundred pounds in a month. She had got bored and called her pen pals, Linda in Australia and Rachel in Chicago, and her cousin Priyanka in India. As a punishment, her parents cut her pocket money and confiscated her mobile phone for a month and even now she wasn't allowed to use their house phone un-supervised.

I switched on my PC and as soon as I logged on to MSN, she popped up!

PartyBharti: Where have U been?

Makdiva: Sorry!

PartyBharti: Come on then, spill.

Makdiva: Well, he has this really cool house. It's kind of.
              What?

I stopped as I could see Bharti was already writing to me.

PartyBharti: If I wanted to know about interior design, I'd
              watch flipping *MTV Cribs*!

Makdiva: OK, OK.

PartyBharti: What did you wear? I hope it wasn't that nasty,
              grey, hooded sweatshirt you claim is from
              America!

Makdiva: It IS from America! No, I didn't wear that. Give
              me some credit.

PartyBharti: I don't think so – I've seen some of the stuff in
              your wardrobe! Now tell me what you wore,
              because I know you didn't take any of my style
              advice.

Makdiva: My black jeans, and black top.

PartyBharti: Whaaaaaaaaaat? Are you crazy? That would
              have made you look like you were going to a
              funeral! I hope this guy isn't a Piscean cos
              they're very sensitive to auras and colours.

Makdiva: LOL! I wore black jeans, my pink V-neck
              jumper and my funky scarf from Camden
              Market.

PartyBharti: Phew! I got stressed there. What about ear-
              rings?

Makdiva:	Obviously the ones from Accessorize!
PartyBharti:	I hope you mean the pink ones and not the crystal chandelier ones that should only be worn at parties?
Makdiva:	Yeah!
PartyBharti:	That's all right then. What about shoes?
Makdiva:	Ohmigod, what is this – the fashion police interrogation special or something?
PartyBharti:	Just tell me!
Makdiva:	Trainers.
PartyBharti:	Would it have hurt you to wear shoes?
Makdiva:	U know I can't walk in heels! Imagine if I'd stomped around in them and fallen over!
PartyBharti:	What, like you did last year at Nick's birthday party? LOL!

I walked straight into that one. Nick's birthday party was fine when I sat down, but dancing in those shoes nearly killed me. I lost my balance and, had it not been for his brother, Paul, I would've fallen into the birthday cake! Not that I minded being rescued by Paul, it was the humiliation of everyone else knowing I couldn't walk in heels that added to my pain.

Makdiva:	It wasn't LOL, it was painful!
PartyBharti:	2 ur EGO!
Makdiva:	That's it, I'm signing off!
PartyBharti:	OK, I'll stop. So did you find his place all right?
Makdiva:	No, I nearly missed the stop.
PartyBharti:	U LIE!

Makdiva:	Nope. I pressed the bell, got up and the driver kept on going! All I could see was Nelson's horrified face as the bus whizzed past him at the bus stop.
PartyBharti:	What happened?
Makdiva:	Well, I raced to the front of the bus and pressed another bell and luckily it stopped. Talk about embarrassing!
PartyBharti:	Uh huh!
Makdiva:	Bharti! A bit of sympathy please?
PartyBharti:	I swear my fingers slipped! It is a bit funny though?
Makdiva:	No. The driver told me I should've pressed the bell earlier! Then this old lady got up and had a go at him, because the bell wasn't working. I jumped off as soon as he opened the doors.
PartyBharti:	Where was Nelson?
Makdiva:	He was there. He ran after the bus!
PartyBharti:	Really? That's sweet. A total RM. I wonder what star sign he is.
Makdiva:	I don't know yet. Anyway he hugged me.
PartyBharti:	Ohmigod, physical contact before the date? That means you guys are going to get married or something! Did you wear any perfume?
Makdiva:	Er yes, I nicked a bit of my mum's. ☺
PartyBharti:	Smart move.
Makdiva:	He said I smelled familiar.
PartyBharti:	So quick, tell me what happened!

Makdiva: Well, he showed me around his house. What now?

I stopped because Bharti was writing again.

PartyBharti: OK 1 more time: I DO NOT CARE ABOUT INTERIOR DECORATING!

Makdiva: Fine, no need to shout! We watched this really old film called *TeenWolf* and we had popcorn.

PartyBharti: Any lip action?

Makdiva: No, can you wait?

PartyBharti: Hmm . . . did he?

Makdiva: LOL NOT! We went to his bedroom and played on his PS2.

PartyBharti: Ohmigod! You went to his bedroom? Why? Isn't that like going too far on a first date?

Makdiva: I don't like him that much! I never sat on his on bed or anything! We were on his floor, playing a game.

PartyBharti: Phew! It's weird enough having a first date at his house, but taking you to his room too?

Makdiva: Bharti it wasn't like that! You're as bad as Tanisha! He explained he ran out of money because it was his sister's birthday and he spent his money on her present this month. That's why he couldn't ask me to the cinema or anything.

PartyBharti: OK, I suppose that's a good excuse.

Makdiva: It's good enough for me.

PartyBharti: So then what happened?

Makdiva: Well, we kind of had a popcorn fight after I thrashed him on his favourite game. I'm so glad I spent last summer hanging out with Nick.

PartyBharti: That's a point. I never did work out how you got Nick away from his books and smoothie-making equipment and glued to his PS2!

Makdiva: Can we get back to my date?

PartyBharti: Yeah yeah.

Makdiva: So then I saw his hand reaching for my face and . . . What?

I could see Bharti was typing again so I stopped.

PartyBharti: LOL! I bet you were like totally freaked out and said, 'What are you doing?'

She was right, of course. It was weird to see his hand coming towards me. For a moment I thought I was in trouble and would have to put him in an arm lock, as per Tanisha's instructions and then kick him in the shins. But I wasn't sure how to do that lying on a carpet.

Makdiva: OK I was, but only for a split second, I swear! Plus Tanisha had taught me self-defence moves.

PartyBharti: LOL! So then what happened?

Makdiva: He pulled out a piece of popcorn from my hair.

PartyBharti: LOL!!!

Makdiva: OK, so I didn't need to put him in an arm lock!

56

PartyBharti: Stop it! I can't laugh any more, my stomach aches!

Makdiva: Anyway, then he told me how nice my hair was.

PartyBharti: Oooh, so it was worth getting your braids done on Friday?

Makdiva: Definitely! I didn't even mind the trek to South London this time!

PartyBharti: Well, was there any lip action?

Makdiva: No.

PartyBharti: Ohmigod, he doesn't fancy you!

Makdiva: What, seriously?

PartyBharti: Makeeda, how many boyfriends have I had? I'm messing around? Joke?

Makdiva: You still give good advice and I'm sure you'll get a boyfriend soon.

I knew how sensitive Bharti was and I honestly couldn't see why she wasn't getting asked out all the time with her huge eyes and pretty face.

PartyBharti: Thanks for the sympathy.

Makdiva: I mean it! It's not sympathy!

PartyBharti: Let me know when you find a boy who wants to go out with a size sixteen, five foot five, fourteen-year-old!

Makdiva: Stop it. What about that guy at the Tube station last week?

PartyBharti: He was a foot shorter than me and, ooh, at least thirty years too old for me!

Makdiva: LOL! OK, bad example!

PartyBharti: Thanks Miss un-matchmaker. Get on with the date.

Makdiva: Fine. We stared at each other, then we kissed just as his dad walked in.

PartyBharti: Stop it – U LIE!

Makdiva: Nope. His dad walked in and introduced himself, then told us to go downstairs.

PartyBharti: Whaaaaaat?

Makdiva: Well, like you and Tanisha, he didn't trust us alone in his son's bedroom!

PartyBharti: SEE!! I mean, oh shame!

Makdiva: Yeah, thanks, Bharti! So we hung out watching a film on TV, then he called a cab for me.

PartyBharti: Is that it?

Makdiva: Yeah, well he gave me kiss for about a second on his doorstep as the cab pulled up and the driver hooted his horn.

PartyBharti: Are you for real? 2 interruptions?

Makdiva: YES!

PartyBharti: OK, no need to shout. Well, what kind of kiss was it then?

Makdiva: Which one?

PartyBharti: The first one, of course! The second one doesn't count.

Makdiva: Nice.

PartyBharti: Don't make me come round and slap it out of you. I WANT DETAILS!

Makdiva: Oh, OK then. It was really soft.

PartyBharti: Any tongue action?

Makdiva: Yes.

PartyBharti: Ohmigod!

Makdiva: Not for long though as his dad walked in, remember?

PartyBharti: LOL!

Makdiva: Not LOL! Totally embarrassing – my lips were left in the air before I realised we had company.

PartyBharti: Ha. Haaaaaaaaaaaaaaaaaaaaaaaaaaaaaaaaaaaaa aaaaaaaaaaaaaaaa!

I can't believe she just wrote that. Where is her heart? What is taking her so long to reply it's been two minutes!

Makdiva: Bharti?

PartyBharti: Sorry, I fell off my chair and my finger got stuck on the 'a' key.

Makdiva: Liar! There's an exclamation mark.

PartyBharti: OK, but I did fall off my chair. So is that it?

Makdiva: Yes.

PartyBharti: Wow, that's an interesting first date.

Makdiva: Spill it.

I knew Bharti was hiding something.

PartyBharti: Well, you're a Cancerian and according to your sign for Sunday it said, 'A challenging day but a hopeful beginning,' or something like that.

Makdiva: Yeah and what does that mean?

PartyBharti: Methinks the fates conspired against you, but then again you've had Mercury in retrograde for the past few weeks but all that should change.

Makdiva: WHEN BHARTI, WHEN?

PartyBharti: All right, calm down. Um . . . According to this book, in about three years.

Makdiva: WHAAAAAAAAAT?

PartyBharti: I'm soo glad we're not on the phone. I was just messing. Next week, Thursday. Have you told Mel?

Makdiva: No, not yet, she's been busy with the netball try-outs, but you know what she's like: she probably knew he was going to ask me out!

PartyBharti: Hold on, who did he say you smelled like?

Makdiva: What?

I was hoping she'd forget. I really didn't want to tell her.

PartyBharti: You said he said you smelled familiar.

Makdiva: Don't laugh.

PartyBharti: I promise.

Makdiva: His nan.

PartyBharti: Oh OK, that's really cute.

Makdiva: What no LOL! Or ha haaaaa??

PartyBharti: It's not that funny, besides I promised. Er, how old is she?

Makdiva: 70.

PartyBharti: Ha haaaaaaaaaaaaaaaaaaaaaaaaaaaaaaaaaaaaaaaaaa aaaaaaaaaaaaaaa!

Makdiva:	You promised!
PartyBharti:	I had my fingers crossed!
Makdiva:	How's the diet going?
PartyBharti:	Fine, except I fainted yesterday.
Makdiva:	Whaaaaaat? Are you OK?
PartyBharti:	Yeah, my body obviously couldn't take to that one.
Makdiva:	How many times were you eating?
PartyBharti:	Um, one full meal, plus breakfast and some fruit.
Makdiva:	That's crazy!
PartyBharti:	Yeah, but I lost three pounds in a week!
Makdiva:	U R CRAZY GIRL! Bet you were starving all the time – I would be!
PartyBharti:	Of course I was starving! They took me to hospital and this nutritionist had a go at me. So on top of my family she was the fifth person to shout at me.
Makdiva:	Not surprised.
PartyBharti:	I know, I know. It was a stupid diet! It's just that I heard that Amazonian Anoushka did it.

Amazonian Anoushka was the prettiest and tallest girl in our school. She was on nearly all the school sports teams, modelled and got really good grades too. The rest of the school were divided between those who liked her and those who hated her but secretly wanted to be her. I liked her as she used to be my maths tutor before she got too busy with modelling.

Makdiva: Ohmigod! That's rubbish. Have you seen the food that girl eats? She never turns down dessert and always has her five portions of fruit and veg a day!

PartyBharti: I know that now. I'm just going 2 try to eat healthily now.

Makdiva: Finally!

PartyBharti: As soon as we got home, my dad threw away the diet book. He had his suspicions when I turned down my nan's samosas for some salad last Monday.

Makdiva: U TURNED DOWN NANA SUNITA'S FOOD?

PartyBharti: I know! Weird, eh?

Makdiva: More than weird. Your nan's food could outsell every curry house in Brick Lane in an hour!

PartyBharti: I'll tell her you said that! She's here now and I can smell dinner.

Makdiva: Oww, I'm so jealous.

PartyBharti: Come round!

Makdiva: Nah, I've got to catch up with some homework. I spent ages on the history project.

PartyBharti: Who did you choose in the end?

Makdiva: Yaa Asantewaa, the Queen Mother of Edewso in the 1800s who fought the British military.

PartyBharti: Interesting, using Ghanaian history, eh?

Makdiva: Yeah.

PartyBharti: So who told you about her?

Makdiva: Don't laugh, but I found an article in Agoo Magazine.

PartyBharti: Really?

Makdiva: Uh huh.

PartyBharti: Well, at least you've finally handed it in. You took ages finding your topic!

Makdiva: I know! I hope Mrs H likes it.

PartyBharti: She will. It's different. Mine was on Indira Ghandi, Mel did Mary Seacole and not sure who Laura did. Julia reckons it was Mariah Carey but Laura's not that bad.

Makdiva: U never know. LOL! It's good that we all did someone different.

PartyBharti: Definitely. What homework?

Makdiva: Science: do Exercise 4 for Friday. Oh yeah, English: read the next chapter in the novel.

PartyBharti: Cheers. Bye!

Makdiva: Bye!

I clicked out of MSN and wondered whether my date with Nelson had been totally jinxed or not. I guess Bharti was right: it was funny that we got interrupted twice whilst kissing. At least we kissed. But did that really mean he liked me? What if he was being polite or something? Was he really worth lying to my parents about?

Chapter 7

What, No Gold Stars?

We had just spent the past half-hour watching the most boring video on Britain in the 1930s and now knew what life was like before World War Two. The streets looked a bit like the set of *Coronation Street*, but I just kept wondering what the rest of the world looked like.

'Lights,' bellowed Mrs Hipman. She handed out a worksheet based on the video we had just watched.

'This is so boring!' said Mel, as we completed the answers.

'Yeah, didn't you think the streets looked like *Coronation Street*?' Bharti said.

'That's just what I thought!' I added and we all sniggered.

'You two are such Londoners!' Mel commented.

'When is she going to tell us about our projects?' whispered Bharti.

'Good question,' I said.

'Excuse me, I'm talking to you!' boomed Mrs Hipman.

We all jumped.

'Ohmigod! Miss, you scared us,' Mel said.

'Well, whatever it takes to get your attention,' she replied. 'Right, I have your essay plans here.'

An excited buzz immediately fell over the class. We all wanted to know if our plans could be developed into essays. I watched as everyone had their plans returned and realised that I hadn't received mine.

'Brilliant, I can use it!' said Bharti. 'I just have to be careful about listing sources. Where's yours?'

'I don't know. Excuse me, Miss?' I said raising my hand.

'Yes?'

'Um . . . Miss, I haven't got my work back,' I said.

'Oh yes, Makeeda, I need to speak to you.'

The bell rang for our next lesson.

'Right, ladies, I want you to start writing your essays for homework.'

'Yes, Miss,' the others chorused as they rushed out.

'Miss, I'm going to be late for my next lesson,' I said.

I watched as she scribbled on a piece of paper and gave it to Bharti.

'Are you in the same lesson?'

'Yes, Miss,' Bharti replied.

'Give this to your teacher,' she said, shoving the letter in Bharti's hand. 'And close the door!'

'Yes, Miss,' Bharti said, rushing off.

'Take a seat, Makeeda.'

I was actually beginning to wish I was in science with Mrs Connelly screaming at me to pay attention to an experiment.

'I'll come straight to the point.'

Great! I folded my arms across my chest. It was obviously bad news then.

'I don't think you can create an essay using your choice of topic.'

'What? Why?' I said, shocked.

'Well for a start, your grades have been floating between A and C for the past year . . .'

'That's not fair. Everyone's grades are like that, and I've only ever got three Cs, the rest are As and Bs!' I said, standing up.

'Sit down. I just think this essay would be too much of a stretch for you. Besides, you won't be able to find enough resources for Yaa Asantewaa. Pick an alternative subject for your essay. You could do Mary Seacole,' she said.

She's got to be joking! Apart from Mel and me, the other four black girls in our year had probably already claimed that topic as their own.

'Come on, Miss, give me a chance. I can do it!'

'Makeeda, I'm not repeating myself. Choose another topic and resubmit your plan to me by Thursday of next week,' she said, and began sorting out her papers.

'Fine,' I mumbled.

Within minutes I was slipping into a bench station in the science block, next to Bharti and Mel. It was nice having Mel around without Laura. It sounded mean, but I was glad Laura had gone home early for a dental appointment.

'Are you OK?' Bharti asked.

'No, not really,' I replied, before filling them in on all the details.

'Hey, put on your overall before Connelly notices,' Mel reminded me.

'Cheers,' I said, practically emptying my rucksack to find it.

Within minutes, Bharti was pouring a solution into the test tube (that I was holding using tongs) and Mel was using a thermometer to record its temperature before heating. I placed it in the flame of the Bunsen burner as our conversation changed to soap hunks.

'Definitely that really cute guy in the soap about stepfamilies,' I said.

'Who?' Bharti asked.

'The one who plays the older brother,' I said.

'Ohmigod, he's soo ancient!' Mel said, laughing.

'Who are you talking about?' demanded Bharti.

'The guy who played the nerd in that school soap,' Mel explained.

'Makeeda!' yelled Mrs Connelly, rushing towards me.

'Whaat?' I said, confused.

She turned off the Bunsen burner and took the tongs and test tube from me. I noticed it had changed to a weird shade of orange, unlike the test tubes everyone else was holding which were pale egg-yoke colours.

'I can't believe you overheated the solution! That's it, I'm splitting you three up! You're a danger to yourselves and my equipment,' Mrs Connelly exclaimed.

'Sorry, Miss,' we chorused, desperately trying not to laugh. Luckily the bell rang signalling the end of the day.

'Clear off the lot of ya!' Mrs Connelly shouted, but most of the class were already out of the door.

'Hey, are you two coming to the netball trials?' Mel said.

'Er no,' I replied.

'Hey, wait up!' Laura screamed, as she ran up to us.

'What are you doing here?' Mel said, smiling.

'I wasn't going to miss the trials. I would've been here earlier, but I couldn't be bothered to go to history or science. So I hung out with Jordan and Nelson. They finished early today.'

Nelson? What was she doing with him?

'Ready?' Laura asked Mel.

'Yeah, I was just trying to convince these two to come along,' Mel said.

'Oh,' Laura said, surprised.

'The last time we were on the team, I got disqualified for elbowing the Wing Defence in the eye and Makeeda sprained her ankle chasing that girl from St Mary's,' Bharti said.

'Don't remind me!' I said, wincing.

Every time I thought about that particular match, I recalled the agony of landing in a funny way and thinking I was going to die from the pain.

'Oh yeah, I remember your starring moment ruined by a sprained ankle!' Mel said, laughing. She hooked her arm in mine and made me run ahead of the other two.

'So how are things with Mr DJ?' she asked.

'OK. We're meeting up at the weekend.'

'Ah huh, the second date! Excited?'

'Well, not really – more nervous . . .' I began.

'Hey, did I tell you I heard that Nelson once dumped a girl for being a poor kisser?' Laura called from behind us.

'What?' Bharti said, horrified, looking at me.

'That's rubbish! He's not like that!' Mel said.

'Well, it's what I heard!' Laura added, staring directly at me, her eyes shining.

The others waited for me to reply, but I had nothing to say. I was in shock. What if Laura was right? I mumbled my good-byes and almost ran out of school.

'Hey, wait up!' Bharti called, huffing and puffing for breath. 'What was all that about? You know Laura's just winding you up.'

'I know but . . .'

'Makeeda, what's up?'

'I'm worried that Nelson will dump me on our second date.'

'Er, why?'

'Because . . . because . . .' I couldn't think of what to say.

'Because you have bad taste in nineties rock music, which you always deny? Or because of your weird sardine, onion and ketchup sandwiches?'

'Shut up!' I said, laughing.

'Don't worry about it. You'll be fine. Mercury comes out of retrograde tomorrow.'

'Really?'

'Yes, so you should be OK!' she said, unconvincingly. 'Although . . . I foresee dark clouds brewing above Laura,' Bharti added.

'Really?'

'Nope, she's a Gemini – they're always lucky!' Bharti said with a smile.

We kept talking till we saw a good-looking boy waiting at the bus stop. He was about Nelson's height and had the same school uniform on.

'Ohmigod! I think I'm in love,' Bharti whispered.

Then we both shut up. Judging by the silly grin on her face, Bharti was locked in a fantasy world with our unknown companion, whilst I was still concerned about my second date with Nelson. Laura could actually be right and Nelson could be using this second date to dump me for being a poor kisser! My mind drifted between Nelson and my history essay. There was no way Mrs Hipman was going to make me write about someone else. I'd never got into an argument with a teacher before, but there was something about Yaa Asantewaa that made me want to fight.

Chapter 8

It's All About the Second Kiss

I'd been stressing about this date for days. So far, the closest Nelson and I got to a second kiss was when he met me at the bus stop, and that was a peck on the lips. I was beginning to think that he really was going to dump me.

We jumped off the bus and began the walk to the music shop in Edgware.

'You don't mind, do you?'

'No, it's fine,' I replied.

'I just prefer this shop to the big chains. It's just as good,' Nelson said, staring at me. I smiled back.

Actually I was impressed. I mean I never think about stuff like that. Bharti and I always head for the coffee shop that's part of a chain, instead of the smaller one. It just looks more inviting and has real sofas.

We walked past a couple huddled against the wind and my mind drifted back to the all important second kiss. I'd read in one of my magazines that the second kiss counted more than the first, because the first was almost forgotten once it happened. I was also stressing about my essay. It wasn't really easy, but I wasn't finding it a total nightmare either. My only problem was Mrs Hipman's reaction. The essay plan I'd submitted was on Mary Seacole and not Yaa Asantewaa. So I knew I'd be in trouble as soon as she read my title.

'Are you OK?' Nelson asked.

'Yeah, why?'

'Nothing, you just seem to be miles away,' he said.

'Nah, I'm right here,' I lied.

I decided not to tell Nelson about my essay situation. I didn't want him thinking he was going out with a nerd. That's if we were actually going out with each other. Without that second kiss, it was hard to tell.

'Good,' he said, and slipped his hand in mine.

We arrived at the shop and Nelson immediately disappeared into the new releases whilst I just milled around.

'Hey, have you heard this?' Nelson asked, thrusting an old Motown LP in front of me.

'I . . .'

'I love this song!' Nelson said.

I watched as the biggest grin spread across his face and lit up his eyes.

'I haven't heard it before,' I said.

Before I knew it, we were in a sound booth and he'd placed headphones on me. He gently slipped his arms around my waist and I felt his scarf tickle my neck. I was happy, until he kissed me lightly on the lips and I realised it was just another peck. The song began to fade out and I replaced the headphones.

'Well?' he asked, helping me out of the booth.

'It's . . .'

'I love it! It's my favourite song. Well, one of them!' he said enthusiastically.

It was the first time I'd heard him sound so happy.

'I liked it,' I replied.

Instantly I realised that I'd given him a less than enthusiastic response. He just looked at me oddly.

'You don't have to lie. If you hated it, you can say so.'

'No, no, I like it! I just realised that I've heard it before. My dad played it once, but I never knew who sung it,' I said and hoped that it was enough.

'Oh, right.'

'So how come it's so important to you?'

'My mum and I used to sing it to each other when I was little.'

'Oh, right.'

'Yeah, well we used to anyway . . .' he said, then looked away.

'What do you mean?' I could sense that there was more to it, but I wasn't sure if I sounded nosy in asking.

'She and my dad have separated. I live with my dad, and my sister lives with her,' he explained.

'Oh,' I said. I wasn't sure what to do. Do you say I'm sorry to hear that? Anyway, I was a bit weirded out by his dramatic mood swing. I could hear it in his voice.

'I don't miss the arguments or anything, but . . .'

'What?' I asked.

Ohmigod, I'm so nosy! I wish I could stop treating people like characters in a soap!

'Well . . . she never went to my first gig.'

'Really?' I asked, shocked. That seemed really mean but I was hardly going to tell him that.

'Basically, she hates everything to do with my DJing.'

'Wow, that's harsh!' I said. I suddenly realised I'd called his mum harsh.

'I know. She expects me to be all academic like her and my grandfather back in Africa and become a barrister. My sister's doing A-levels so she can study law, but that's not enough for mum: everyone's got to do it!' he said furiously.

I could see that we were beginning to attract some stares from other people in the shop.

'I'm sorry,' I said. That sounded so lame – like something a teacher might say. 'I know what you mean though,' I added.

'I bet your mum's really nice,' he said, giving me a smile.

'She can be, when I'm not around,' I said, thinking about Tanisha.

'What do you mean?'

'Nothing,' I replied.

I'd only ever told Bharti and Nick about the stuff with Mum and even they didn't know the full story. I wasn't comfortable having to rake it all up again.

'Maybe your mum will change her mind,' I said, hopefully.

'I don't think so, Makeeda,' he said, angrily heading to the cashier.

I wasn't sure what else to say. I guess I was confused. How could he be so happy one minute, then sad the next? We left the shop in silence, but he still slipped his hand into mine. I was cold but I was glad I hadn't worn my gloves.

'Hey! You're African!' I said suddenly. It was really high pitched so I immediately cringed.

'Last time I looked, and Brazilian.' He smiled at me again.

'Really?' I asked.

'Yeah, my mum's from Togo and my dad's from Brazil. You're African, right?' he asked.

'Yeah, my family's Ghanaian and a quarter Lebanese.'

'A quarter?'

'Yeah, I have three Ghanaian grandparents and one mixed-race grandmother.'

'Makeeda, that's not a quarter.'

'Yeah, yeah, I know, but a quarter sounds better,' I said.

'You're funny!' said Nelson, laughing.

'Er . . . funny weird, or funny ha ha?' I asked.

'Definitely weird!' he said, grinning.

'So rude!' I said and hit his arm.

'Ouch! I'll get you back for that! Do you want to go to Harrow for something to eat?' he asked, as we approached Edgware station.

'Um . . . yeah, OK. Hey!' He'd just taken my hairband out of my hair.

'Come on, there's our bus!' he said, running ahead of me.

I ran after him and only caught up because there was a queue. Mel might have been right about me needing more exercise.

'Here you go,' he said, giving back my hairband.

I was too out of breath to respond.

'You should leave it down. It looks nice,' he added.

'Thanks,' I replied, but I wasn't taking any chances. The last thing I wanted to do was to whack him in the eye again with my renegade braids.

We climbed the stairs to the upper deck of the 340 and sat at the rear of the bus.

This is it! I thought. Back seat of a bus equals second kiss, (those pecks don't count). Ohmigod, I hope I don't mess this up. What if I bite his tongue or something?

'Makeeda? I . . .' Nelson said, as a woman came and sat two seats away from us.

'Yeah?'

'Um . . . nothing,' he said.

OK that was weird. Why did she have to sit so close? There were like twenty other empty seats and she had to get within earshot of us.

We sat in silence until the woman got off in Stanmore.

'Come here. Why are you sitting all the way over there?' he said and patted the empty seat between us.

Hmm . . . let me see, I thought. I could be annoyed because you don't seem to want to kiss me or just too flaming nervous to sit closer to you!

'No reason,' I lied.

He leaned in close to me and I could feel his breath over my face. My heart was pounding so hard that I actually held my breath. I was surprised: the closer he got, the more his breathing became erratic. My eyes closed and I waited. I felt him pull away, so I opened my eyes to find him looking out of the window.

What was going on with him? I didn't just imagine it – he *was* going to kiss me! So why was he ignoring me?

'Nelson, I ...' I began, but I was interrupted by a voice coming from the stairs.

'Hey, DJ Nelson!' said a mixed-raced boy in a blue puffa jacket and a baseball cap heading towards us.

He was followed by Stephen, the red-haired boy from Mel's party, and a tall, thin black boy dressed smartly in a black coat, trousers and shoes.

'All right?' said the smartly dressed boy, nodding towards me.

I smiled back.

'We weren't interrupting anything, were we?' said the boy with the baseball cap.

'Shut up, Jordan,' Stephen said.

'Why? Isn't she the one ...?' Jordan began.

'Leave it, Jordan,' said the tall thin one.

'All I was going to say was, isn't this the girl Nelson's been ...' Jordan began.

Been what? Had he been talking about me?

'I don't believe it! Jordan man, can't you stop running your mouth for a second?' said the tall, thin boy.

'Makeeda, this is Hakeem, and you've met Stephen, right?' Nelson said.

'Yeah,' I replied, smiling at Stephen.

Jordan coughed loudly.

'Oh yeah, and motor-mouth over there is Jordan,' Nelson said, pointing at the boy with the baseball cap.

'So where are you two off to then?' Jordan asked.

'Harrow,' Nelson said.

77

'Cool, fancy some company?' Jordan added.

'I don't think so!' Nelson said sternly.

'Man, you must have been dropped as a baby!' Stephen said to Jordan.

'What is wrong with you?' Hakeem asked.

'What?' Jordan said, looking confused.

'Would you take your mates along if you were out with your girl?' Hakeem asked him.

'Well . . . they look bored. Maybe I could help break the ice . . .' Jordan began.

'More like shatter it!' Stephen said, making us laugh.

'Shut up! Ginga minger!' Jordan said.

'Here we go,' Nelson muttered.

'Listen, at least when the laydeez see me, they don't forget. You look like every other brother with that hair. Actually scratch that, you wished you looked like every other brother!' Stephen said, swiping Jordan's hat from his head.

Jordan tried desperately to conceal his uneven afro but we'd all seen it.

'That's out of order!' Jordan said angrily.

'Bro, sort that out! Please?' Nelson said, smirking.

'My sister keeps promising to braid it but keeps cancelling,' Jordan moaned.

'Find someone else then!' Nelson said.

'Don't suppose you know how to . . .' Jordan said to me.

'Er . . . no. I don't,' I replied.

I was pretty much hopeless at plaiting hair. Mum tried to teach me using Delphina's hair, but gave up and ended up combing out all the knots my plaits had made. Delphina still believes I did it on purpose.

'Oh, I just thought maybe you'd prefer to run your fingers through a real afro!' Jordan said.

Ohmigod, he's flirting with me! In front of Nelson too!

'I don't think so,' I said.

'You can't say stuff like that to your mate's girl! You were definitely dropped as a baby!' Hakeem said, whacking Jordan's cap.

'You know what, Jordan? With hair as dodgy as that, you couldn't even get a granny to give you a smile,' Nelson said and we all began laughing.

'Hey, it's our stop!' Jordan said, jumping up.

'Jordan, you better not take long. My shift starts in half an hour!' Hakeem said.

'Where are you going?' Nelson asked.

'Oh we're going to find a barber in Wealdstone for Jordan,' Stephen said, making us laugh again.

'Shut up, man. It's not that bad!' Jordan said, racing down the stairs.

'Yeah well, he can't see the bits peeking out below that cap,' Hakeem added.

'I'll give you a shout tonight!' Stephen said, smirking at Nelson. 'See ya, Makeeda!' he added.

'Bye!' Hakeem said, racing after them.

As the upper deck became silent once more, I wondered about Hakeem.

'Hey, how come Hakeem works?'

'Oh, he's sixteen. He has to support his mum and little sister.'

'Oh.'

'His dad left them about two years ago . . .' Nelson began. The noise outside interrupted him.

'Hey, Nelson!' screamed a voice outside.

We stared out of the window to see Jordan.

'Are you two going to snog all the way to Harrow?' he asked.

'Ohmigod!' I said.

'Jordan!' Hakeem said, whacking him on his hat again.

'Ahh . . . come on, you know they want to . . .' Jordan began.

I stared at the huge queue of people getting on to the bus. Some of them were our age and enjoying the scene.

'I'm going to kill him!' Nelson muttered.

'Hey, if you're going upstairs, give the lovebirds some space!' Jordan called out, laughing.

'Jordan man, that's so wrong!' Stephen said, trying to shut him up.

I pulled myself away from the window, closed my eyes and sunk into my seat. I was hoping that my head wasn't visible, even to the people sitting ahead of us. I wanted to die. This was beyond embarrassment. I felt like I was being punished for every single lie I'd ever told.

As the bus pulled away from the stop, I could still hear Jordan shouting.

I slowly opened my eyes and turned towards Nelson. He too had crouched down in his seat – quite an achievement for someone of his height. I could hear the sniggers of a group of girls our age, a few rows ahead of us.

'I am so sorry,' Nelson said, looking at me.

'It's OK,' I said, and he surprised me by giving me a peck

on the lips. It would have been more than that, if we hadn't got the mwah-mwah kissing sounds from the girls sitting ahead of us. Once again, Nelson looked out of the window, while I gave them a dirty look before grabbing my book from my bag.

I was beginning to think that Nelson didn't want to kiss me, when he slipped his hand in mine. He was still looking out of the window, but I saw him smirking at me through his reflection in the glass.

Fifteen minutes later we were standing in the middle of Harrow debating where to eat.

'The Chicken Hut?'

Tanisha had warned me about eating chicken with my fingers on early dates.

'No.'

'Makeeda, where *do* you want to eat?'

'I don't mind,' I said.

I didn't want him to think I was fussy, despite my responses. I could hardly tell him I didn't want to go anywhere I'd spill anything.

'You're not vegetarian, are you?' he said worriedly.

'As if! How many West-African vegetarians do you know?'

'True, my mum and my aunt put meat in everything!' he said, laughing.

'So do mine!' I said, joining him.

My phone rang. It was Mum.

'Hello?' I said tentatively.

This was it. She'd found me out on my second date. I waited for her to start screaming at me. Nothing happened.

'Hello?' I repeated.

'Makeeda, I'm going to text you right now,' Delphina said, immediately cutting off.

'Ohmigod, I'll kill her!' I said angrily.

I totally forgot I was with Nelson.

'What's wrong?' Nelson asked, looking concerned.

'My little sister's just being annoying as usual.'

'What's her name?'

'Delphina.'

'Really? It means Dolphin in Spanish,' he said, smiling.

'Yeah, it was my grandmother's middle name.'

He said something in a foreign language.

'Is that Spanish?'

'No, Portuguese – that's what they speak in Brazil. I speak French too, because of my mum. Togo used to be a French colony.'

'Oh right,' I said.

'Say it after me.' He said something in Portuguese and I repeated the phrase.

'What does that mean?' I asked.

'My boyfriend is gorgeous,' he said, grinning.

'That's so cheeky!' I said, hitting him on the arm.

Wait a minute! That meant that he saw me as a girlfriend, didn't it? But without that second kiss they were just words.

My phone beeped. It said Mum, so I knew it was Delphina.

Mum: Can u buy my Fairytale CD please? You promised!
       Love, your favourite sister, Delphina. X

Me: Fine. Just don't call or text me again today.

I quickly shoved my phone in my bag.

'Er . . . I have to get her something from HMV,' I told Nelson.

I was hoping he'd just think that I meant a poster or something. There was no way I was going to tell him I was buying a Fairytale CD after the way I reacted at Mel's party.

'Oh right. If we go now, we can chill and eat before we go home,' Nelson said.

'OK,' I said smiling.

We headed back to the shopping centre and narrowly avoided being separated by a group of Italian students in brightly coloured winter jackets and huge rucksacks. Nelson's grip on my hand tightened until we were standing safely in HMV.

As I looked across the shop, I began to regret teasing him at Mel's party.

'So what are you going to buy?' Nelson asked.

'Oh um . . . a CD for my mum. It's a surprise,' I lied.

'Yeah, which one?'

'Oh um . . .I've forgotten the name,' I said, avoiding eye contact.

'Hold on, you've got to buy a CD, but you've forgotten the name of the artist?'

'Uh huh,' I said.

Just let it go Nelson.

'What about the title?'

'Um . . . nope.'

'What about the colour of the sleeve?'

Oh flaming hell! He would decide to be helpful, wouldn't

he? My fault for going out with a DJ.

'You know what? I'll just call my mum and ask.'

'I thought you said it was a surprise?'

For crying out loud!

'Er . . . I meant I'll call Delphy. Why don't you look around, it won't take me long,' I said, hoping he'd take the bait.

'OK, if you're sure,' he said with a shrug.

I headed towards the rock section and pretended to call Delphina. Then, I made sure he wasn't looking, which wasn't hard given the way he towered over the racks of CDs, and I grabbed the Fairytale CD. I held it low, against my thigh. When I looked up, Nelson was smiling at me.

Crikey, he knows! I thought, but he went back to flicking through some CDs, so I rushed to the queue, nearly colliding with a security guard.

'Watch it, love!' he said.

'Sorry,' I replied.

I paid for the CD and turned around to find Nelson waiting for me by the door.

'Finished?' Nelson questioned.

'Yeah,' I said, stuffing the CD into my bag.

'You know what? That security guard was following you around the store.'

'Really?' I said in disbelief.

Ohmigod, I'm not a thief.

'Yeah, it was really weird. I guess he thought you were trying to steal something.'

Great! Now I'm going to be followed every time I go in there, all because of a Fairytale CD! I could kill Delphina!

'You know, you did look kind of shifty . . .' he said, smiling.

'Hey!' I said, laughing nervously.

'So what did you get?'

'Oh um . . . The Fusion Funksters,' I lied. That was an old group Dad liked.

'Oh right.'

'You know who they are?'

'I'm a DJ, Makeeda?'

'Oh yeah, of course,' I said, feeling stupid.

'I'm kidding. My dad has their album too and plays them when he's dropping me off at my mum's. Can we eat now?'

'Yep! Let's go to the café over there!' I pointed, and this time I grabbed his hand and led the way. By seven o'clock we'd finished eating and I had managed not to spill my food everywhere.

We still hadn't had our proper second kiss, but I wasn't as stressed about it. After Jordan's antics and managing to hide the Fairytale CD, I was feeling really chilled out. I still had half an hour to get home; my curfew was eight p.m. but Tanisha told me to get home half an hour early, as apparently parents love it. I wasn't convinced that mine would even notice because of their radar for my lateness, but I decided to go with it.

I turned to Nelson. We were sitting on my bus home, as he'd insisted on at least taking the bus back with me.

'Thanks for coming with me,' I said, smiling.

'I wanted to,' he said, smiling back. 'Besides, after all that stuff with Jordan, I had to make sure you didn't bump into him again.'

'True,' I said.

We got off the bus and Nelson pulled me into a doorway.

'I wanted to, um . . .'

'Yeah, whaaat?' I said, confused.

He surprised me by kissing me.

'Oh!' I said, pulling away.

Crikey, he's going to think that I'm weird. I wait all day for it, then I pull away.

'What's wrong?' Nelson said, concerned.

'Nothing, I just wasn't, um . . .' I stuttered.

'Didn't you want to?' Nelson said apologetically.

'No, no, I did . . . I just . . .' I leaned towards him and this time I just relaxed.

Wow! Now that's what I call a second kiss.

My phone rang.

'Um . . . hello?' I said, flustered.

'You OK?' Tanisha said.

'Yeah, yeah,' I said, giggling.

'OK! Well, I'm waiting for you at the bus stop. Hurry up, I'm freezing!' Tanisha said.

'Yeah, yeah, OK,' I said, and hung up.

'Who was that?' Nelson asked.

'My cousin. I've got to go now.'

'Oh right. Well, I think I'm entitled to one more kiss.'

'Yeah?' I said, smiling.

'You know, seeing as I had to wait all day . . .'

'There you go!' I said, pecking him on the cheek. Two can play your game, mate!

'Is that it?'

'Yep!' I said, as I began walking away.

'Hey wait! Can't I walk you home?'

'No, it's OK. My cousin's just over there,' I said, as I pointed ahead of me.

I didn't want to tell him that my parents would kill me if they found out about him. I looked at my watch. It was half past seven, so I started to run. Nelson began chasing me down the street and caught me by the waist.

'Can I call you tomorrow?' he said, breathlessly.

'You ran after me to say that?' I asked. Or maybe he wants to kiss me again, I thought.

'Well, yeah,' he said smiling.

'OK. Um . . . you can let go of me now,' I said with a grin. He let me go.

Ohmigod, why did he let me go? Didn't he want to kiss me?

'OK, well . . . bye then!' he said, waving awkwardly.

I guessed not.

'Bye!' I said, but neither of us had moved.

We were staring at each other. He had amazing eyes, even without the contacts in; they were an unusual light shade of brown, compared to his deep skin tone.

We probably would've kissed again, if it hadn't been for Tanisha running up to us. That would have made our third real kiss. I guessed that would have to wait till our next date. If my parents didn't find out first.

Chapter 9

Makeeda's Online Community

I threw my notepad on to my bed and chewed the end of my pen. I was really glad that I hadn't just regurgitated pages from a school library book. Instead, I was learning about an amazing woman from Ghanaian history. It was weird. I was actually enjoying the assignment and, at the same time, I felt like I was connecting with my Ghanaian culture. My only problem was that I'd hit a wall. I couldn't seem to understand the real reason Yaa Asantewaa went to war. I was beginning to wonder if Mrs Hipman had been right about me not finding enough information. My phone beeped twice.

Bharti: Get on MSN now!

Nick: Have u finished your essay yet?

Me: I'm stuck so I'll have a break.

I switched on my computer and logged on, and a window popped up. Initially I wasn't sure who it was.

PrincessBhartilina: What took you so long?

Makdiva: Why have you changed your MSN name?

PrincessBhartilina: Hmm . . . let me think. I should be royalty and my parents should have named me Bhartilina! Good enough 4 U?

Makdiva: OK, crazy gal! So what's up?

PrincessBhartilina: You have to help me get Hitesh's attention!

Makdiva: Er, how? He's your brother's best friend. You should have it all sorted by now.

PrincessBhartilina: Listen, Miss I-had-a-fantastic-second-kiss, we don't all have your hot lips you know! Don't you want to help me? ☹

Makdiva: OK, OK, no need for the emoticons. When's the next time you're going 2 see him?

PrincessBhartilina: Um . . . Actually, I was hoping you could help me with that 2.

Makdiva: What?

PrincessBhartilina: Tejas is going away on a field trip and I have to pick up his homework from Hitesh. Could u come with me? PLEASE?

Makdiva:	OK, when?
PrincessBhartilina:	Monday B4 school.
Makdiva:	Whaaaaat? That means I have to get up early!
PrincessBhartilina:	You agreed! Besides, you're not the only one due some romance this month. So what's the plan and make it romantic!
Makdiva:	OK, calm down. Let me think about it.

<MELodrama online>

MELodrama:	Hiya girls.
Makdiva:	Hey, Mel, how do you get an older guy's attention? We need some help.
MELodrama:	I thought you and Nelson were OK?
PrincessBhartilina:	Not for her, for me!
MELodrama:	Oh right. Well, they don't like girly stuff like chocolates and CDs and kind of laugh if u spend all your pocket money on a fancy watch.
Makdiva:	Ouch.
MELodrama:	Yeah, yeah, I learned the hard way. So listen up.

Another window popped up on my screen.

MrSmoothie:	All right?
Makdiva:	What do you want, Nick?
MrSmoothie:	Shouldn't u be writing that essay?
Makdiva:	OMG! Is it not enough that you have to tutor me? Now you want to make me

	study 24/7? I said I was having a BREAK!
MrSmoothie:	Stop being a drama queen! So who are you chatting to?
Makdiva:	Not telling!
MrSmoothie:	Why, is it your boyfriend?
Makdiva:	No Bharti and Mel actually.
MrSmoothie:	Invite me in then!
Makdiva:	No! ☺
PrincessBhartilina:	Thanks, Mel!
MELodrama:	Makeeda, where have you been?
Makdiva:	Just getting rid of Nick! Hey how did the netball trials go?
MELodrama:	I got in!
Makdiva:	Really? That's great!
MELodrama:	I know, it makes it easier to do GCSE PE coursework. Laura got in too.
Makdiva:	That's nice.
MELodrama:	She's not that bad, Makeeda.
Makdiva:	Not to you she isn't.
MELodrama:	U and Bharti should try out for the new football team.
Makdiva:	U do remember the last time we were on a team, right?
MELodrama:	Yeah, I was thinking that all that aggression would be great on a football pitch.
MrSmoothie:	Actually, Mel, Makeeda'd probably get enough red cards to cover her bedroom walls! ☺

PrincessBhartilina:	LOL.
MELodrama:	LOL.
Makdiva:	For crying out loud, Bharti! Did you have to invite him?
PrincessBhartilina:	Stop being mean to Nick. He's lovely.
MrSmoothie:	Yeah, Makeeda, stop being mean to me. I'm lovely. ☺
MELodrama:	You two are like an old married couple; we can't split you up.
Makdiva:	Whatever!

A new window popped up. It was Nelson.

DJNelson:	Hey!
Makdiva:	Hey yourself!
DJNelson:	So what are you up to?
Makdiva:	Chatting to you . . .
DJNelson:	Ha ha ha! So when can we meet up again?
Makdiva:	I've barely recovered from our last meeting.
DJNelson:	Really? I thought we had some unfinished business. You still owe me a kiss.
Makdiva:	Nah, I think you'll find you're the one with the debt, mate! So what are you doing today?
DJNelson:	I'm at my mum's and avoiding her.
Makdiva:	Why?
DJNelson:	Oh, just the usual.

I wasn't sure how to reply to that. I mean, I completely understood what he meant, but I didn't want to have to explain why. The window of the other conversation was flashing.

Makdiva:	Nelson, you'd better join my other conversation.
DJNelson:	OK, I will. I'll be there in five.

PrincessBhartilina:	Where have u been, Makeeda?
Makdiva:	Hey! I was chatting to Nelson. ☺
MELodrama:	You're not the only one with a love life, you know. I saw Jason yesterday.
Makdiva:	What as in saw him drive by the bus stop or something? ☺
MELodrama:	Ha ha, you're so funny. No, as in I spent the day with him.
PrincessBhartilina:	Am I the only one not in a relationship? ☹
MrSmoothie:	You and me babe!
MELodrama:	Hey, r u asking Bharti out, Nick?
Makdiva:	Yeah?
MrSmoothie:	I didn't mean it like that.
PrincessBhartilina:	Heartbreaker!
Makdiva:	So annoying, isn't he?
MELodrama:	He's such a playa. Bharti, you're well rid of him!
MrSmoothie:	Oh thanks!
<DJNelson online>	
DJNelson:	All right?

MrSmoothie:	Who are you?
MELodrama:	Shut up, Nick, you know it's Nelson!
MrSmoothie:	Right, Mel, that's why I asked!
MELodrama:	Ahh, Nick's put out because he's not the only guy in Makeeda's life!
PrincessBhartilina:	Mel!
MrSmoothie:	You're talking rubbish.
DJNelson:	What's going on?
PrincessBhartilina:	Nothing. Just ignore them.
MELodrama:	Nick, just admit it. You're jealous!
MrSmoothie:	I AM NOT JEALOUS, MEL!
PrincessBhartilina:	Whoa, no caps in this conversation pls?
MELodrama:	Whatever! I don't want to talk to you any more, Nick.
MrSmoothie:	Fine by me, Mel!
DJNelson:	Are they arguing over me?
PrincessBhartilina:	No, Nick's Piscean like me, and Mel's Leo. It's kind of inevitable really.
DJNelson:	Oh OK then.
MrSmoothie:	Mel's obviously been repressing her feelings for me, but you know what? Sorry, hon, you're just not my type!
MELodrama:	I'll repress u in a minute!
PrincessBhartilina:	LOL nice1 Nick! U2 Mel!
MrSmoothie:	I thought u weren't talking to me???
DJNelson:	Bharti, R they always like this?
PrincessBhartilina:	Sometimes.
Makdiva:	OMG can't you 2 pretend to be normal?
MrSmoothie:	Normal is boring, Makeeda!

MELodrama:	You should know, Nick!
PrincessBhartilina:	Ouch!
DJNelson:	LOL!
MELodrama:	Oh and Nick, your smoothies don't taste that gr8, so I'd change your MSN name!
PrincessBhartilina:	Mel!
Makdiva:	That's not true, Mel!
MrSmoothie:	Mel, why don't u just !@*$ off!
Makdiva:	Nick?

\<MrSmoothie logged off\>

Since selling those recipes to the supermarket, Nick had been trying to come up with some more, but now everyone was making smoothies, so it had become more difficult. Delphy kept telling him to diversify or something.

PrincessBhartilina:	OMG MEL!! He never swears! That smoothie comment was so out of order!
MELodrama:	Whatever!

'Makeeda?' Mum yelled.

Makdiva:	Back in a sec!

\<Makdiva away\>

I ran out of my room and raced downstairs to talk to Mum. Five minutes later I returned to find Delphina sitting at my table, typing away on MSN.

'What do you think you're doing?' I asked, surprisingly calmly.

'I'm just chatting to your friends,' Delphina said, still tap-tapping away.

'You don't have to hammer at my keys like that! Just move before I call Mum. If I catch you in here again, I'll destroy your blue collection.'

Delphina had two collections of hair bobbles and hairbands – one was blue, the other was pink. She gasped in horror and ran to her bedroom.

Makdiva:	I'm back! Sorry that was Delphy before. Don't worry, I'll scroll up and find out what was said.
DJNelson:	Hmm . . . u do that!
PrincessBhartilina:	Your sister has just outted you!

I looked at the screen and couldn't believe it. In the space of a few minutes, Delphy had destroyed any street cred I had!

MELodrama:	I always knew you liked Fairytale!
DJNelson:	At least now I get why you were so weird in HMV. Pretending not to know the name of the CD? We'll talk later, Makeeda!
PrincessBhartilina:	Ooooh, sounds like someone's in trouble!
Makdiva:	Nelson? What does that mean?
DJNelson:	U'll have to wait and see! ☺ Later Bharti, Mel!

<DJNelson logged off>

Makdiva:	Gr8! ☹
MELodrama:	I invited Laura.
Makdiva:	Uh huh.

I was furious that she was in our conversation.

PrincessBhartilina:	How's the essay going, Makeeda?
Makdiva:	It's all right. I've just got one bit to sort out, that's all.
LushLaura:	Isn't it a bit risky, choosing a topic like that?
Makdiva:	Actually, I'm not afraid of a challenge, Laura.
MELodrama:	Well, mine isn't exactly a breeze.
PrincessBhartilina:	Tell me about it!
LushLaura:	Mine isn't hard.
Makdiva:	Is that why you chose it?
PrincessBhartilina:	You know what? I think I will try out for that football team.
LushLaura:	Are you saying I'm thick? At least I'm not in the lower set for maths.
MELodrama:	That's a good idea, Bharti. How about you, Makeeda?
Makdiva:	Yeah? Well, why don't you !#*$ off into someone else's conversation!
PrincessBhartilina:	OMG!!
LushLaura:	This from a girl good at English?
MELodrama:	Leave it, Laura.

97

LushLaura: U lot bore me!
<LushLaura logged off>
PrincessBhartilina: What's with the language today?
MELodrama: I dunno.
<Makdiva logged off>

I was so furious I shut off MSN altogether. I needed to sort
out my essay anyway and there was only one person who
could help: my grandmother, Nana-Amma in Ghana. She used
to be a headmistress, so maybe she could tell me a bit more
about Yaa Asantewaa. I decided to call her.

I usually messed up the pin codes on the phonecards. Mum
would kill me if I didn't use them though.

'Hello?'

'Good evening,' Nana-Amma said.

'Can I speak to Nana, please?' I knew it was her but I had
to be really polite or she'd tell me off.

'Speaking. Makeeda, is that you?'

'Yes, Nana,' I said.

'How are you?'

'Fine, how are you?'

'Well, I've just come back from a funeral in Accra. How are
Delphina, Tanisha and Nick?'

As far as I could tell all Nana-Amma seemed to do was go
to outdoorings and funerals.

'Yeah, everyone's fine. I really need your help though.'

'OK.'

'I'm writing an essay about Queen Mother Yaa Asantewaa
and I'm stuck on . . . hello?' I said.

'Carry on, I'm here. I'm curious, Makeeda.'

That's not such a good thing. Nana-Amma's curiosity was usually followed by a question or statement that made you look stupid.

'Why are you writing this essay?' she asked.

'It's for a history assignment on inspirational women,' I said.

'So your teacher asked the entire class to write an essay on Yaa Asantewaa?' Nana-Amma questioned.

'Well . . . no, not exactly, Nana.' I told her how I was writing it against Mrs Hipman's wishes.

'Makeeda, you still haven't answered my question. Why are you writing this essay?'

'Oh . . . I don't know, she sounded really interesting. A brave, inspiring woman, who fought to protect our identity,' I said.

'Are you reading that from a book?'

'No!' I said, shocked. I put the book down. 'OK, maybe the brave bit, but I thought of the rest myself,' I said, making Nana-Amma laugh.

'Oh, Makeeda!' she said. I could hear the happiness in her voice. 'Right, what do you need to know?'

I told her about my confusion over Yaa Asantewaa's true motives for going to war.

'Why are her motives so important?' Nana asked. 'You should also be discussing her legacy.'

'What do you mean?'

'Well, think about it. She may not have won the war, but she must have achieved something, Makeeda,' Nana-Amma said.

'Nana, she ended up in exile with Asantehene, King Prempeh I, and all the other chiefs, including her own nephew.'

'I know all that, Makeeda!' Nana-Amma said. 'Now, start thinking about her legacy and you'll understand exactly what I mean,' she added.

'Can't you just tell me?'

'No. Then, I'd be doing this essay for you, wouldn't I?'

'I suppose,' I said. I hate it when she does this.

'You can do this, Makeeda. Keep going and show that teacher of yours!' she said.

'OK, but can I call you when I've finished?'

'I want a copy of your essay when you've finished! You can bring it with you at Christmas . . .'

Whaaaat? I'm not going to Ghana for Christmas.

'Don't you mean Tanisha, Nana?'

'I'm not senile, Makeeda! I want you to come to Ghana over Christmas with Tanisha. Think about it.'

'Um . . . OK. I'd better go now.'

'Fine. Tell Nick to call his Nana-Betty. She said he hasn't called in ages.'

'I will. Say hello to her from me. Thanks, Nana. Bye'

'You're welcome,' she said, hanging up.

Ghana? Ghana? What's going on? That came totally out of the blue! If I don't mention it, maybe Mum and Dad won't either. I don't want to go to Ghana for Christmas! Ohmigod! That would mean leaving Nelson. I mean what if he said he wouldn't wait for me?

Chapter 10

Baby Akosua's Outdooring

I stepped out of the car and stared at Delphina. She was wearing the same ntoma as me and we looked awful in my opinion. It was always better when we weren't wearing the same fabric. The ntoma was lilac and pink and, whereas Delphy's had been cut into a simple dress, mine was in a top that had huge lace cuffs that kept getting in my way and a skirt that was difficult to walk in. I knew I'd be fine as long as I didn't have to move my hands too quickly – there was a small risk of me becoming airborne if I did. Thankfully, Mum was not happy with my ntoma either and vowed to speak to the tailor in Ghana.

I looked across at Mum. Under her coat, she was wearing ntoma in the style of a loose lemon dress, with a matching duku that was criss-crossed across her head. Dad was wearing a shirt of white fabric over trousers and his best shoes. It had just stopped raining, so we were all dodging the puddles and clutching our coats just that little bit tighter against the cold weather. We walked up the road passing clusters of houses until we reached the loudest one, Uncle Larry and Aunt Anita's place. The sheer volume of noise seemed to envelope us well before we reached their open door.

We walked in and were greeted by Aunt Grace, who was wearing pink lace in the style of ntoma.

'Thank goodness you're here. We can start now,' Aunt Grace said rushing back in.

'Oh no, the time!' Mum said, realising how late we were. 'I'm so sorry.'

'Mummy, it's eleven-thirty. Why was Aunt Grace worried?' Delphy asked, puzzled.

'Your aunt was just concerned because we never perform the ceremony in the afternoon and they were running out of time,' Dad interrupted.

We entered the room and shook everyone's hands, starting from those sitting on the right side of the room. I looked up and Afua was smirking at me, waiting for me to shake her hand.

'Nice outfit,' she whispered, then sniggered.

Great, that's all I need. Afua is a petite girl who always looked sophisticated wearing ntoma. She never gets it wrong and that day was no different: she wore pale blue ntoma in the style of a simple A-line dress. Her family took her everywhere, so she could speak in Twi effortlessly. I heard a rumour that she could also speak in another Akan based dialect, but I was hoping that wasn't true. Everyone our age envied Afua's linguistic abilities because it meant that she could understand what the adults were saying. Who wouldn't want to know in advance whether to avoid their parents? She wasn't exactly my favourite person to hang out with, but we kept getting lumped together because we're the same age. I'm not even sure if we're related, but I'm praying we're not.

I took my seat on the floor next to Delphy, in front of Mum and Dad, as all the adults and Afua had taken up the real seats. I looked over and saw Uncle Larry and Auntie Anita smiling broadly as they handed over their daughter, Baby Akosua, to Aunt Grace. She was going to conduct the ceremony. Uncle Larry was Dad and Aunt Grace's cousin, their fathers were brothers.

Aunt Grace began her speech and then called on Delphina to help.

'Me?' Delphina said, surprised.

'Go on,' Mum said, poking her in the back.

I watched as Delphina stood up and went to Aunt Grace's side. Auntie Anita placed a silver tray with four silver cups in her hands. I saw Delphina peering into them and looking confused. I knew what they contained, because I had to carry them for Delphina's outdooring. They were in pairs: salt and sugar, water and vodka (or some other clear alcohol). When I asked what they symbolised, Mum told me it was for the baby to recognise the difference between right and wrong. I kind of thought it also meant let your words be sweet when needed and bitter or strong when needed, but I never told anyone because they'd just laugh.

I watched as Aunt Grace spoke in Twi before dipping her finger into one of the cups and gently placing it just inside Baby Akosua's mouth. She repeated it for three cups, then went to the last one, and we all saw Baby Akosua's tongue clearly lick the vodka off Aunt Grace's finger. Baby Akosua's grandmother said something to Aunt Grace in Twi that made everyone laugh.

'It looks like Baby Akosua definitely knows the difference between water and alcohol,' Mum whispered to me.

'Oh,' I said, smiling. 'A bit like Delphy and sugar?'

Mum laughed. 'Yes,' she replied.

Delphina did the same thing with sugar at her outdooring, which probably explained her love of sweets. I looked up and saw Aunt Grace holding Baby Akosua up in the air and saying her full name.

'Sarah, Jessica, Akosua-Serwah, Boakye. Akwaaba!'

Everyone began cheering and clapping and I overheard Mum whispering in English to Baby Akosua's mum.

'Sarah Jessica?' Mum asked.

'Yes, what's wrong with that?' Aunt Anita replied. She ignored the look of disbelief on Mum's face.

'You really miss that TV show, don't you?' Mum questioned.

Ohmigod, Baby Akosua was named after an actress?

'Sister, you know as well as I do that custom doesn't let mothers choose names for their children. Fathers do,' Aunt Anita said, smirking.

'Ha!' Mum said, laughing. 'You know how to influence the outcome though.'

Aunt Anita laughed, as I quietly slipped away from the celebrations and headed for the stairs, armed with my mobile.

As I sat down, Delphina raced towards me.

'Makeeda, hide me!' she said.

'I don't think so.'

'But I'm your sister!' Delphina pleaded.

'And?'

'You're so . . .' she began, but then she raced upstairs.

'Delphina, Delphina? Even though you cheated, I forgive you,' Kofi shouted.

'You?' I said, horrified.

What was wrong with this kid? Why was he still hanging around with Delphina after their last fiasco? A few months ago, Delphina had convinced him to ask me out, in exchange for a five pound note. My sister effectively pimped me.

'I don't suppose you'd reconsider?' Kofi said, sitting beside me on the stair.

'Reconsider what?' I asked, just as he placed his tiny hand on my knee. 'You'd better move your hand before I whoop your ass!'

'Just checking. I don't go out with girls in braids anyway.'

'How old are you?'

'Ten and a half.'

'Great, take your ten and a half self and . . .'

'Hiya, Makeeda,' said a woman dressed head to toe in black and white Kente. 'I see you've met my son.'

'Yes, Auntie,' I said, faking a smile.

'Seeing as you two get on so well, I might have to get you to babysit.'

I don't flaming think so, love!

'Well, I think Delphina gets on really well with Kofi, so . . .'

And I hope she cons him out of all his pocket money, I added mentally.

'There you are!' Kofi interrupted. He had spotted Delphina at the top of the stairs.

Luckily Kofi's mother was called away and the gruesome twosome left the stairs and headed to the dining room.

I switched on my phone, expecting at least one message from Nelson, but I had one from Bharti and Mel. I decided to reply to Bharti's first.

Bharti: W R U?

Me: Outdooring with that 10.5 yr old wannabe playa, Delphina tried to pimp me out to.

I decided to read Mel's whilst I waited for Bharti.

Mel: OMG W R U? Laura's dad is driving us down to Chessington and said she can invite her mates.

Huh? That made absolutely no sense. Laura and I aren't mates, so why was Mel telling me this?

Me: I'm at an outdooring! Can't escape, so have a good time. Er, tell Laura I said thanks for the invite.

I waited two minutes before Bharti replied.

Bharti: Oh shame! Has he tried to make u play kiss chase yet?

Me:	Shut up! What r u up 2?
Bharti:	I'm meant to be helping mum with some cooking for the Festival of Light.
Me:	Diwali!
Bharti:	Yeah, which means I get to hang out with my bitchy cousin Meena who got 10 A*s and is so pretty she was in a Bollywood film. I'm over it. She was an extra and had only one line. Besides it was filmed in Wembley which is definitely not LA or Bollywood.
Me:	LOL!
Bharti:	So we're still on for Operation Hitesh tomorrow?
Me:	Yeah, I'll meet you at the bus stop near their school.
Bharti:	Gr8! Gotta go, gran alert!

I didn't have time to ask Bharti whether she got an invite to Chessington before receiving another text message.

Nick:	How's it going? Have you managed to come up for air yet?
Me:	Where do u think I am?
Nick:	Somewhere with wassaname.
Me:	His name is Nelson.
Nick:	Whatever. Have u sorted out that essay yet?
Me:	Ohmigod, it's Sunday morning, Nick! Get a girl-friend and stop being so weird!

I deleted the girlfriend bit and put in 'life'. Even I couldn't be that mean. The last girl he fancied was only interested in his brother Paul. My phone beeped just as I was about to put it away but I didn't recognise the number.

Anon: Makeeda, I invited you because your boyfriend is
        going. Laura.

How did she get my number? Stupid question really. Maybe she was being nice. Ohmigod what's going on, Laura's being nice?

'Makeeda?'

I looked up to see Mum standing over me.

'Mum?'

'What are you doing here?' Mum asked.

'Oh . . .' I began.

I couldn't tell her I'm bored because she'd get really angry.

'I wasn't feeling well,' I finally managed.

'Oh, so text messaging your friends has helped?'

I was stuck. I couldn't think of anything to say. Besides, how long had she been standing there? Had she seen any of my text messages about Nelson?

'Right, can you go and help your Aunt Grace in the kitchen, please?'

'Yes, Mum.'

I headed for the kitchen and found myself watching Afua smiling and helping to serve rice into a huge bowl.

'Glad you could join us, Makeeda,' she said under her breath.

'I'd stop talking. Your breath reeks of garlic – been tasting the food?' I countered.

I saw a look of complete horror cross her face as she immediately excused herself for the bathroom.

'I heard that,' Aunt Grace said from behind me.

'I . . . I . . .' I stuttered.

I didn't want to get into any more trouble.

'Take this into the living room and pass it round.'

'Yes, Auntie,' I said, taking the tray of *atwimɔ* and tit-bits. The *atwimɔ* were fried biscuits cut into tiny golden squares and were on the left side of the tray whereas the titbits consisted of strips of pastry with peanuts and raisins. I re-entered the living room and went around with the tray and napkins, when I was stopped by a woman dressed in a mint-coloured ntoma that was covered with yellow flowery patterns.

'Hello,' she said.

I saw a glint in her eye. Here it comes, the usual mini test in Twi that I always fail.

'*Yɛ frɛ wo sɛn?*' she asked

Hold it, I know this one. It's . . . how old are you? No wait, it's . . . I've got it! It's 'what's your name?'

'*Yɛ frɛ me* Makeeda,' I said hoping for the best.

'*Ei Makeeda ni?*' she said, shouting and smiled and then grabbing me by the shoulders. Luckily Auntie Anita took the tray from me before I showered everyone with *atwimɔ* and tit-bits.

'Do you remember me?' she asked.

I hate that. If you can speak to me in English what the hell is the Twi test about?

'Um . . .' I wondered.

I could just be honest and say no, but I've done that before. It doesn't work and I end up looking rude. I'm expected to remember people I met when I was two; end of story. No consideration given for the fact that they may have changed hairstyles quite dramatically like jerry curl or wet look to anything decent.

'Of course she does, Auntie Felicia!' Mum said, suddenly standing behind me. 'Makeeda, you remember the little boy you used to play with in Ghana?'

'Er . . .' Of course I don't, Mum.

'The one with the toy lorry you used to fight over? Isaac?' Mum added.

Ohmigod, him? That kid made my life a misery when I tried to play with that toy. I was only in Ghana for two weeks and I had to spend three days at his house.

'Isaac! Yeah, sure,' I replied, giving my best fake smile. 'Ouch,' I added, as Mum gave me a none too subtle poke in my back, whilst pretending to adjust my ntoma.

'This is his mother,' Mum said.

'Hello, Auntie,' I said, almost giving a genuine smile.

'Makeeda, *wo ho te sɛn?*'

I don't believe it. Is it not enough that her evil son made my life hell for three days; she's still testing my Twi?

'*Me ho yɛ*, Auntie,' I replied.

That's it. My Twi is limited to 'My name is Makeeda' and 'I'm fine'. So this is the point I dread, because I just won't understand the next question and it's unlikely she'll ask for my name again.

'So how is Isaac?' Mum asked.

Saved by my mother! That's when I switched off and excused myself. I was just about to run and hide, when I literally bumped into Afua.

'Watch it!' Afua said.

'Like I would intentionally bump into you, Afua,' I replied.

'I heard you trying to speak Twi.'

Great! That's all I need.

'What exactly is an outdooring?' Delphina interrupted. 'Kofi says it's the same as a christening.'

'How come you're asking me?' I said suspiciously.

Kofi was standing three feet away from us and pretending badly that he wasn't listening to our conversation.

'No reason, I just thought you'd know,' Delphina said.

'Listen, Makeeda, if you don't know, I don't mind explaining it,' Afua said.

Ohmigod, why can't I just hit her and be done with it?

'No thanks, Afua,' I said angrily. 'Kofi is right in a way, as it is a naming day. The thing is, we don't perform this in front of the Christian God, unless we're in church,' I began.

'Makeeda, they're not going to understand the difference between pagan and Christian rituals!' Afua interrupted. 'Listen, all you need to know is that a long time ago, way before Ghanaian people believed in a Christian or Muslim God, they named their babies and introduced them to the world by holding an outdooring.'

It's not fair. Why couldn't I explain it like that? I looked at my sister, the traitor.

'Oh, OK then,' Delphina said, smiling.

'Is that it?' Kofi said, piping up.

'Yes,' Afua said, allowing a smug grin to crease her face.

Then I saw it. The look in Delphina's eye that usually means nothing to anyone else, but I know as 'I haven't finished yet'.

'You know, you didn't really answer my question, Afua. I mean, we still don't know what the differences between an outdooring and christening are. Thanks anyway though,' she said.

Afua stared at her in disbelief, whilst I watched the best little sister in the world run off with her latest sidekick.

'You know, both of you were right,' said Aunt Grace, from behind us. We both spun round.

'Thank you, Auntie,' Afua said, almost smiling.

Great! I can't even enjoy myself without her spoiling it for me.

'Can you two help me in the kitchen, please?' Aunt Grace asked.

'Sure, but I have to leave in half an hour,' Afua replied brightly.

Even Afua has a decent escape route.

'Something wrong, Makeeda?' Aunt Grace questioned.

'No, Auntie,' I replied hastily.

I spent the next hour helping Aunt Grace, who rewarded me with fried plantain that was sweet, soft and juicy. Unfortunately I had to share it with Delphy and later Tanisha, who arrived with so many bags of shopping that Dad made us put them in the car before she greeted all the guests. Tanisha was excused from the ceremony because she wasn't related to Baby Akosua's family.

'Ohmigod, the woman is impossible!' Tanisha moaned.

'Who?'

'Our grandma! She wants me to take some stuff out to Ghana for her.'

Tanisha was leaving the next day to start her voluntary work in our grandmother's old village.

'Makeeda, I've been all over Oxford Street for the clothes

and kitchen utensils, East Street Market for her tights and then Kilburn for her hair stuff!'

'Oh,' I said, trying not to snigger.

'Plus, I did this all without a car, on a Sunday! It's crazy!' Tanisha said, literally throwing the bags into the boot.

'Come on, I'll get you some rice,' I said, throwing my arm across her shoulder.

I went straight to the kitchen and got Tanisha some food, whilst she went around greeting everyone. Although none of the people were relatives from her side of the family, most of them knew her.

I walked into the living room to a buzz of Twi and people staring at her excitedly.

'*Ei Tanisha ni? Wo maame wo hen?*' said an elderly woman.

The room went silent. I knew '*maame*' meant mother. I looked around and couldn't see Mum, Dad, Aunt Grace, or Auntie Anita or Uncle Larry. Tanisha was alone. I was rooted to the spot. I wanted to do something to help, like usher Tanisha away, or explain to the woman that Aunt Jennifer had died, but the words just wouldn't come. I felt guilty. I knew I was betraying my cousin.

'She died,' Tanisha replied.

'*Kosɛ Nyame wɔ hɔ!*' the elderly woman added.

It was a phrase I'd heard Aunt Grace use often. It meant something like: 'My sympathies, God is there for you.'

Suddenly Dad was there, whispering to Tanisha, and she left the room.

'Makeeda, go and sit with Tanisha,' Dad said.

I nodded and he smiled.

We sat in the corridor in silence. I wanted to tell her that it was OK to cry but, because I still felt so jealous of her relationship with Mum, I couldn't bring myself to.

I was still clutching her plate of food, minutes later, when Delphy and Kofi came strolling up.

'Mum said you have to get our coats,' Delphina said.

'Oh,' I said.

I didn't want to leave Tanisha but then I saw Mum heading our way. When I returned, Tanisha was almost herself again. I couldn't help but feel left out when I saw Mum hugging and whispering to her.

We said our goodbyes and drove home. Tanisha was staying with us before leaving for Ghana. The only conversation in the car was between Dad and Delphina. I looked between Tanisha and Mum, who were silently staring out of the car; both thinking about the same person. Dad later told me that the old woman at the party had no idea that Auntie Jennifer had died.

Just before we got home my phone beeped.

Mel: OMG we are having a wicked time! Nelson and Jordan are really funny. I c y u like him. Laura's been keeping him company as they both love rollercoasters. Wish u were here. X

Oh great. That's all I need.

Chapter 11

School Run – Makeeda Style

I stared at Mum. She was dressed in a navy blue trouser suit and cream blouse. I noticed that she had on the earrings Dad had bought for her fortieth birthday and was wearing a lot more make-up than usual. Something big was going on.

'Did you hear me?' she asked.

'Er . . . I have less than forty-five minutes to get ready for school, and you want me to take Delphy by bus?'

'Yes.'

'Great!' I said, hiding under my duvet. Usually Mum drove us to Wealdstone where she dropped Delphy at school, while I caught the bus into Harrow.

'Makeeda, now! And don't wake Tanisha up,' Mum said,

ripping the duvet off the bed and leaving.

I looked over at Tanisha, fast asleep in the fold-out bed on the other side of my room. She was leaving for Ghana that night, so was spending the day doing last-minute shopping then hanging out with us after school.

'Fine,' I said, and stormed off to the bathroom.

I had no idea what was going on and, to be honest, Mum's attitude had killed off any curiosity I had.

Around forty-five minutes later, Delphy and I were chasing after the 186 bus. Surprisingly, it wasn't packed, so we were able to get seats next to each other.

'Makeeda, can I have some of the sweets you've got in your pocket, please?'

'How did you know?'

I reluctantly pulled out my pack of strawberry-flavoured lollipops. I was strictly a chocolate girl, but Tanisha had bought them for me as it reminded her of the summer we spent in Brighton as kids.

'Actually, I'll let you have them if you tell me what Mum's up to.'

'OK,' Delphina said, placing a hand over the bag. 'Well . . .'

I could see her grip tightening, so I tightened mine. I don't trust my sister.

'Makeeda?' she said, realising I wasn't quite ready to let go. 'Tell me then.'

'OK, she's thinking of teaching history . . .'

'Where?' I said loosening my grip.

Mum had done a PGCE a year ago and the first thing I did at her graduation was make her promise never to teach at my school. I remember she smiled.

'At some college in Manchester,' Delphy said, successfully snatching the bag from me.

'You're lying!' I said, mortified. 'That would mean we'd have to move.'

'It's our stop,' she said, getting up.

As we started walking towards Delphy's school, my mobile beeped with a message.

Nelson: Meet me in twenty minutes in McD's for breakfast. Wealdstone. I haven't seen u in ages. :(

This had to be a joke. Although it was on my way to school, I didn't like the way he asked.

'Who's that?' asked Delphy.

'None of your business,' I said.

Me: OK

I agreed to meet him because I felt guilty about not being able to see him over the weekend.

'Well, tell me about Mum then.'

'She had a meeting with her boss.'

'Is that it? Why did you lie to me?'

Delphina just shook the bag of lollies in my face and grinned.

'Whatever,' I said.

My phone beeped again. This time it was Bharti, but I didn't open it as Delphina's tie distracted me.

'Did you tie this yourself?' I asked.

'Yes,' she said, pushing my hand away from it. 'Shouldn't you see who your text is from? I can do it for you,' Delphy said, reaching for my phone.

'Nice try, Delphy,' I said, turning my phone off.

'But there's nothing wrong with my tie,' Delphy moaned.

'It's terrible! If Miss Greenwood sees it, she'll make you redo it in front of your class.'

I wasn't lying. She was a mean woman and I'd seen her do it to a girl in my class when I was Delphy's age.

A panicked-looking Delphina stared back at me.

'Come here, then,' I said and redid her tie on myself, then placed it over her head and tucked it behind her dark green pinafore.

'Thanks, Makeeda,' she said, smiling. 'I'm sorry I lied.'

'What are you up to? You never apologise,' I said suspiciously.

'Do you have change for a pound?' Delphina asked.

'Yes,' I said, waiting until she gave me the pound coin first.

'Thanks,' she said, smiling as she placed the change into a small plastic box.

'Fess up or I'm telling Mum . . .'

'Oh look, there's Daniel!' she said, racing off through the school gates.

I knew she was up to something but I didn't have time to find out.

I walked down the road to McD's to find Nelson in a sweatshirt and jeans, sitting in the corner with Jordan and Laura who were in their school uniform. What are they doing here? I wondered.

'Hey, Makeeda!' Jordan yelled, calling me over.

'Hiya!' I waved to them, giving a smile.

'Morning,' Nelson said, standing up to kiss me on the cheek.

At least he and Jordan were pleased to see me. Laura gave me a dirty look. I added my coat to the pile stacked up between Jordan and Nelson.

'How come you're not going to school?' I asked.

'Oooh . . . Someone's in trouble,' Jordan said, in between mouthfuls of pancake.

'Shut up, Jordan!' Nelson said. 'I just didn't fancy it today.'

'Oh right,' I said. I thought it a bit weird but, then again, I really didn't want to look a nerd.

'Hey, how come you didn't come to Chessington with us?' Jordan asked me.

'I . . .'

'Makeeda obviously had a better offer,' Laura interrupted.

'I had a family thing to go to,' I replied.

'Yeah, Mel told me,' Nelson said.

'Sounds like you two don't talk to each other much,' Laura added.

She had a point. Nelson never told me about going to Chessington, Mel did. It felt like he wasn't really bothered about me not being there. He invited me here and didn't tell me we wouldn't be alone. Plus, I didn't tell him about the out-dooring.

'Hey, remember when we got chucked off that ride?' Laura said.

'Yeah, and you got into an argument with that guy and we

all had to leg it before the security men caught us!' Jordan added, and they all fell about laughing.

'What about Mel throwing up after that rollercoaster?' Nelson added, causing more laughter.

I was surprised as she could usually handle the fastest rides.

'Uh huh, she was all, "I can handle anything", then started throwing up after the ride,' Jordan said, laughing.

I smiled, but I didn't laugh. It really annoyed me that I couldn't share in the joke and Laura knew it. I looked at my watch; I had ten minutes to get to school. I didn't fancy catching the bus with Laura.

'I'd better go,' I said suddenly.

'Can't you stay for a bit? Do you want a drink?' Nelson asked.

'No, I can't miss school. I've got to see my history teacher.'

'Oh right,' he said, heading off to the counter.

'Can't you be late?' Laura asked.

'I already am. Aren't you going in?' I asked her.

'I've got a dentist appointment at eleven so I won't get in till, oohh, after midday!' she said smiling and flicking her hair. Laura was queen of the well-timed hair flicks.

'Nice!' Jordan said, impressed.

'See ya!' I replied.

I expected Nelson to follow me, but he was still at the counter so I left.

I had reached the bus stop when he came running after me.

'Why didn't you say goodbye?' he said.

'You seemed busy.'

'Are you pissed off with me?'

'No. Not really,' I lied.

I didn't want to come across as needy or anything, but I did want to see him alone. Plus we hadn't spoken or text messaged each other in ages.

'Yeah you are. Is it because of Chessington?'

'No,' I lied.

'I wanted to see you this weekend, Makeeda, but you said you were busy.'

'I know, but I just thought . . . I thought that you invited me here because we hadn't seen each other over the weekend!' I said, slightly louder than I would've liked. I was angry because he didn't seem bothered.

Nelson didn't respond immediately, instead he looked away from me. I suddenly felt nervous. Was he going to dump me for being too clingy?

'You're right,' he said. 'It would've been better if it was just you and me.'

'Yeah,' I said and, to my relief, he smiled at me.

'I, um . . . missed you . . . I mean it was rubbish without you there,' he said, looking embarrassed.

'Yeah?' I said, smiling.

'Yeah. I mean, I don't know if you'd pretend to like roller-coasters, like your mate Mel,' he said, grinning.

'Ohmigod! That's so rude. FYI – I love rollercoasters.'

'I don't believe you,' he said, so I hit him on the arm. 'Do you want to meet up later? I could come to your house for a change?'

'Um . . . it's not a good idea. My cousin's leaving for Ghana tonight, so we're having a family night,' I said.

'Oh, right.'

He was clearly disappointed, but there was no way I was going to let him anywhere near my house – or, more importantly, my parents.

My bus pulled up alongside us and I made my way to the queue.

'I'll text you later,' he said, kissing me on the cheek.

'OK.'

I took my seat and saw him staring back at me from the pavement. He looked odd standing there dressed casually amongst commuters in coats and smart clothing. I could see that he was cold as he wasn't wearing his jacket, but it was the way he was staring at me that unnerved me. It made me think that he could see straight through me. Like he knew that I was lying to my parents, and that was why I never invited him to my house. The bus pulled away and he waved goodbye but I was left feeling guilty.

I managed to slip into assembly next to Bharti, giving my form tutor the excuse of waking up late. She must have been in a good mood because she didn't give me the usual automatic detention.

Bharti barely looked in my direction, until we were heading back to our form rooms for our first lesson.

'Bharti?' I said, grabbing her arm.

'What?' she asked.

'What's up?'

'Nothing.'

'Hey, Makeeda, have you seen Laura?' Mel asked.

'Yeah, she was in McD's with Nelson and Jordan this

morning. She said she had a dentist appointment.'

'Oh. Is she coming in today?' Mel queried.

'Yeah, about lunchtime,' I replied.

'Oh right,' Mel said, shrugging. 'Was Jordan alone?'

'Yeah, apart from Nelson and Laura,' I told her. 'Why are you so worried about Jordan?'

'Great! Well I hope it was worth it, Makeeda!' Bharti said, storming off to our first lesson.

'What is her problem?' I asked.

'I dunno, but I've never seen her like that,' Mel said.

I spent the day being ignored by Bharti. It wouldn't have been so bad if we weren't in every single class together. I tried everything, even sending notes to her in English, which Ms Ali confiscated. It wasn't until lunchtime that I realised what I'd done. I switched on my phone to find four missed calls from Bharti and three text messages.

Bharti: Makeeda W R U?

Bharti: OMG U R still coming right?

Bharti: Makeeda, I can't believe you've done this to me. I've just had to walk into that college alone to meet Hitesh.

No wonder she hated me! I couldn't believe I'd forgotten Operation Hitesh. Having to take Delphy by bus and then seeing Nelson had made me forget. I decided to reply to her anyway.

Me: Bharti, I'm so sorry. x

I tried to speak to Bharti in the afternoon but, whenever I approached her, she ignored me and even managed to swap seats with Julia for the remaining lessons of the day.

At four o'clock, I saw my opportunity and raced up to her as she was putting on her coat.

'Bharti?' I said, but she turned away from me. 'Bharti, please?'

'What?' Bharti spat out.

I was too shocked to reply straight away. It was something about the way she was looking at me – a mixture of hurt and anger. I knew I had totally messed up, but suddenly I wasn't so sure she'd ever really forgive me.

'Makeeda, what do you want? I need to catch my bus,' she said coldly.

'I . . . I just wanted to say I'm sorry. I totally forgot and I shouldn't have . . .'

'Finished?' Bharti interrupted.

'Yeah.'

That was it. Bharti walked away from me.

'Ohmigod, Makeeda, I've never seen her do that,' said Mel, from behind me. I hadn't even noticed her and Laura.

'I know.'

'You'll sort it out in no time,' Mel told me. 'I've got to go, Makeeda,' she added apologetically.

'Maybe you just need to treat your friends better?' Laura commented.

'What?' I said, turning towards Laura.

'You know, the ones you've got left,' she added under her breath.

I glared at her but said nothing. She was the one person guaranteed to make my day worse.

I just wanted the day to end, but I still had Tanisha's farewell dinner and an airport run to get through.

Half an hour later, I arrived at my front door to the sounds of Tanisha's favourite Motown song, blaring out from the stereo in the living room. I walked in, and Tanisha jumped forward and began lip-synching to the opening words, whilst holding one of Delphy's old toy microphones. Then Delphy herself jumped forward and lip-synched the next line of the lyrics, before they both thrust their mikes in front of me to join in. Which I did, but I was laughing so hard that I tripped and made us all fall to the ground. Mum and Aunt Grace walked in just as we hit the chorus loudly.

We had Tanisha's favourite dinner: spicy mashed potatoes and fish fingers. She surprised us with her choice, but not Mum. It wasn't until Delphy asked that I realised Auntie Jennifer used to make it. Dinner seemed to end almost as soon as it had begun, and within an hour, Tanisha had said goodbye to Delphy and Aunt Grace and was in the airport with Mum, Dad and me, dumping her suitcases on to a trolley.

'You haven't left any scissors, nail files, tweezers, or anything like that in your hand luggage, have you?' Mum asked, as we joined the check-in queue.

'No, Auntie. I came to London from the States!'

'You won't believe who I've just seen!' Dad said excitedly.

As usual, he had bumped into an old friend. Flights to Ghana always ended up being a reunion of some kind, even for those who weren't travelling, as far as I could tell. The last time

Nana-Amma visited, she bumped into an old school friend she hadn't seen in twenty-five years!

'Tanisha, where's your passport?' Mum asked.

'I had it somewhere . . .' Tanisha said, looking in her hand-bag.

'Oh no,' Mum cried out.

'I've got it,' Dad said, patting his top pocket.

Tanisha and I began laughing. We knew Dad had her pass-port.

'That's not funny!' said Mum .

'You know, I've been thinking. We could always join Tanisha in Ghana for Christmas,' Dad said wistfully to Mum.

'I've wondered about that for a while, but what about the garage?' Mum said.

'I'm sure Kyle could manage the place . . .'

'Are you serious?' I said, horrified. I had thought that if I didn't mention what Nana-Amma had said, then there was no chance of Mum and Dad bringing it up. Boy was I wrong! There was no way I was going to Ghana for Christmas. How could I leave all my mates? More importantly, what would happen to my relationship with Nelson?

'You'd love it, Makeeda!' Mum said.

'Yes, you could meet all your cousins and see your grand-parents,' Dad added.

'I don't . . .' I began.

'Let's get a drink, Makeeda,' Tanisha said, practically drag-ging me away.

'Don't go too far away,' Mum said.

Tanisha and I headed to the café.

126

'Right, what's up? I can't leave without knowing who put that sad look in your eyes.'

'I . . .'

''Fess up, Missy! I know it's not just the idea of going to Ghana,' Tanisha said, staring me down.

I told her everything about Bharti.

'Feel better?' she asked.

'Not really.'

'Well, I'm not surprised – the guilt you have . . .'

'Tanisha, where's my sympathy?' I interrupted.

'Listen, you didn't kill her family, or steal her boyfriend. Bharti will forgive you. Eventually,' Tanisha said, shrugging.

'Great, so what do I do till then?' I asked.

'I'd leave it for a few days, then try again.'

'Tanisha!' Mum yelled.

Minutes later we were saying goodbye to Tanisha. I watched as she clung to Mum. There were tears streaming down their faces. I was really sad to see Tanisha go, but part of me was desperate to reclaim my mother.

Chapter 12

Makeeda's Warning

I had spent a total of two hours at the library: one hour researching my essay on Yaa Asantewaa and the other in a maths lesson with Nick. As I walked alongside him to the bus stop, I couldn't help wondering about Bharti. It had been three days since I apologised, but she was still ignoring me at school and hadn't returned any of my messages. I'd met Nelson after school and he'd told me not to worry. He said that Bharti just needed time to be angry and that she'd talk to me afterwards. Nelson even offered to speak to her, but I knew he'd be the last person she'd want to talk to. Besides, he didn't know Bharti like I did. This was huge. I'd totally messed up.

'Makeeda, what's up?' Nick asked.

'Oh nothing,' I said.

I knew he'd be on Bharti's side if I told him.

'Come off it! You were actually paying attention in my lesson and didn't touch your magazine.'

He was right. My magazine still had the transparent plastic over it, sealing the free lipstick. I'd left it untouched for thirty-eight hours.

'Is it Nelson?' he asked. There was a slight tinge of anger in his voice, which I didn't understand.

Our bus pulled up and we raced to the top deck. Nick sat in front of me and turned towards me. He seemed to take up every bit of space in the seat with his stuff.

'Well?' he asked.

'No, it's not Nelson. What's your problem with him anyway?'

'Nothing. I just don't want him messing my cousin around. That's all,' Nick said, looking away.

I smiled. Although I knew we weren't cousins, it felt good to have someone on my side.

'It's Bharti,' I said. Then I told him about our argument.

'Are you mad? You can't be missing school for him.'

'Yeah, I know. That's why I went in,' I replied. 'You're going to take Bharti's side, aren't you?' I added.

'No, but she has a right to be pissed off, Makeeda.'

'I know,' I said.

'I'm going to talk to her,' Nick said.

'What?' I said, astonished.

Nick never ever interfered in what he labelled 'girly stuff', so left any minor disagreements between Mel, Bharti and myself well alone.

'Yeah, she shouldn't be blanking you for this long. It's not important enough to fall out over.'

I coughed.

'What?' he asked.

'Remember when Mikhail added too many blueberries to your banana surprise smoothie?'

'Yeah?'

'You didn't talk to him for nearly two weeks!'

'That was different. I was trying to impress the café owner in Edgware. Besides, that was business.'

'He was still your friend though.'

'Do you want me to help, or not, Makeeda?' he asked.

'Fine.'

'Isn't this your stop?' Nick said, ringing the bell for me.

'Ohmigod!' I said, racing downstairs. 'See ya! Oh and thanks.'

'I haven't called her yet!' he yelled back.

I walked home feeling slightly better and was surprised when Dad didn't shout at me for eating my dinner with my school uniform on. We were in the dining room. He was reading a car magazine and drinking a beer.

'Did you go to the library?'

'Yeah, then Nick came and we did some maths.'

'Good,' Dad said, peering at me from behind his glasses.

Everything changed the minute Mum walked in. She was wearing Dad's sweatshirt and jeans.

'Makeeda, can I have a word?' Mum said, throwing her keys on to the coffee table.

I noticed that Dad quickly made himself scarce.

'Your friend left this for you today,' she said, handing back my scarf.

'Oh right, thanks,' I said, taking it from her.

I suddenly remembered asking Nelson to put it in his bag for me as I was too hot to wear it when we were in a café.

'Nelson. Who, apparently, is your boyfriend,' she added, just as I was about to leave the room.

I stood still.

Ohmigod, ohmigod, ohmigod! This is it! I'm officially making tomorrow's newspapers. I'm a dead girl!

'Anything you want to tell me?'

'Well . . .' I began.

I had no idea what my next words were going to be. Somehow I didn't think that Mum would fall for the old 'he's just a friend' routine.

'Makeeda, do you know what it was like to be told by your daughter's boyfriend that he even existed?' Mum questioned.

'Mum I . . .'

She ignored me and carried on speaking.

This was a total nightmare. I could feel myself getting angrier.

'What do you have to say for yourself?' she interrupted.

'Well I . . .'

Once again she interrupted me.

This was ridiculous! The woman wouldn't even let me speak.

'You've lied to us! I can't believe you've been lying to us. How can we trust you again?'

'Mum, I'm sorry,' I began, but she raised her hand and I stopped. For a moment I actually thought of bursting into laughter. The whole thing was just so stupid.

'How long has this relationship being going on?'

I couldn't believe the way she spat out the word 'relationship'.

'About a month —' I said.

'What?' she bellowed.

'What's the big deal? Auntie Angie let Mel have boyfriends nearly two years ago.'

'You're not Mel and she is not my daughter. We have different rules, Makeeda,' Mum said.

'Ohmigod! It's not like my grades have changed or anything.'

'No, but they haven't got any better either! Oh and if you think I don't know about last week's late mark, then you're mistaken.'

I couldn't help it, I rolled my eyes.

'Don't you roll your eyes at me, young lady! Who do you think you are?' Mum said, raising her hand.

I knew I'd gone too far as she came close to hitting me.

'Go on then!' I whispered. I'm not sure why I said it.

'Makeeda, if I thought hitting you would solve this . . .' Mum said, sitting down. 'Why didn't you tell me?'

'I never told you, because your precious Tanisha told me not to!' I shouted. I couldn't believe how wrong Tanisha had been.

'What do you mean by "precious Tanisha"?' Mum said, standing up.

'You know, the daughter you wish you had!' I screamed at her.

'Makeeda!' Dad said, looking from Mum to me again, as he

came into the room.

I ignored him and carried on.

'The one you prefer spending all your time with! The one you never ignore!' There were tears streaming down my face.

Mum just stood there, staring at me with the strangest look on her face. It was a combination of extreme anger and devastation.

'Oh God,' Dad whispered.

'You always —' I began

'That's enough, Makeeda. Go to your room,' Dad said.

'But . . .'

'Now!' he said angrily. 'We'll finish this discussion later.'

As I left the room I turned to look at my mother. Her expression hadn't changed much, except now she was sobbing in my father's arms. For the first time in a long time, I felt different. I felt lighter. I guess I'd just had enough of lying and pretending that everything was OK, because it wasn't. It hadn't been for ages. I knew I'd just broken every single rule my family had, but I felt strangely calm.

Chapter 13

Locked up

It had been less than twenty-four hours since Mum and Dad found out about Nelson. As it wasn't the holidays Mum and I avoided each other pretty well. Dad drove Delphy and me to school and, unlike Mum, he actually dropped me off outside the gate. That was when he told me that I was grounded until further notice and forbidden from seeing Nelson. I was also told to be home straight after school, which wasn't exactly difficult as the only person I usually hung out with was still refusing to talk to me. I wasn't surprised by the punishment, as I'd answered back and shouted at them, not to mention the real issue: Nelson. I'm not sure how long I actually believed I could get away with lying about him, as well as lying to him.

I spent the day too depressed to attempt an apology to Bharti and, to her credit, she actually sat beside me for all our

lessons and was civil. I was dying to tell her about everything,
but I knew better, so I went to find Mel for some advice. She
was heading to a lunchtime detention with Laura, for arriving
late two days running, when I finally caught up with her.

'Sorry, I can't talk now. Text me,' Mel said.

'But aren't you going to detention?' I asked.

'Yeah, but we've got old Maggie. You know what she's
like.'

'Oh, OK,' I replied.

Maggie was a teaching assistant, who was basically holding
out for her last day. As long we weren't tearing each other's
hair out, she let us do what we wanted in detention.

So I was forced to send Mel text messages.

Mel: Tell him.

Me: Whaat? He'd dump me.

Mel: Yeah and?

Me: I like him, I like having a boyfriend??

Mel: Seriously, Makeeda, just be str8 with him. Tell him
why you're grounded. Tell him everything. Oh + make
up with Bharti, PUHLEASE?

Me: Yeah, OK. I'm working on it.

Mel: OMG psycho student French teacher is taking over,
L8R! x

Wow, I felt sorry for Mel – if Mademoiselle Badeau was taking
over, she'd end up doing French during detention.

I headed off to the school library and made notes on Yaa
Asantewaa. I still hadn't understood what Nana-Amma meant

about Yaa Asantewaa's legacy, but I was determined to work it out.

By the end of the day I'd even managed to get Bharti to walk to the bus stop with me. She was still holding a fantasy book, despite agreeing to walk with me. It was a threat, as I knew if she got truly pissed off with anything I said, she wouldn't hesitate to ignore me and delve into her book.

'Bharti, I'm sorry. I shouldn't have forgotten.'

'Yeah, Nick said,' she replied.

Her words stung. I felt like nothing I said would work.

'Seriously, I'm sorry,' I said.

'Do you have any idea what it was like for me to go to that college without back-up? Those guys are like skyscrapers compared to me let alone the fact that when I saw Hitesh I tripped and went flying into a group of girls.'

I laughed then immediately stopped, unsure of myself.

'Makeeda, it's not funny. I nearly died of embarrassment. It would've been easier if my best friend had been with me,' Bharti said, but she was smiling.

'Yeah, I know. Friends?' I said eagerly.

'OK,' she said.

I hoped that things would return to normal and we'd spend the journey checking out boys from the local school, but it didn't. Instead, we sat in silence until my stop. Bharti only looked up from her book to say goodbye to me. I got the impression that things would be different between us from now on.

I got home and my mind shifted to Nelson. How was I going to tell him that I couldn't see him? I switched on my computer and went straight to my essay on Yaa Asantewaa. An hour later my phone beeped.

Nelson: MSN chat now!

I smiled and logged on.

DJNelson: Whaaaaaaaaaaassup baaaaabe????
Makdiva: I'm OK. I made up with Bharti ☺
DJNelson: Nice 1!
Makdiva: Yeah, Nick had a word, which must have worked.
DJNelson: Oh, so Cousin Nick to the rescue, eh?

Oh great! Yet another person who believes Nick and I are related! I decided not to correct him. After all, my 'cousin' had saved my friendship. I hoped Nelson wasn't annoyed that I got Nick to talk to Bharti instead of him.

Makdiva: It's not like that; he knows her.
DJNelson: Yeah, I know. I'm just messing. So what do you want to do this weekend?

I couldn't tell him the truth – he'd be hurt.

Makdiva: U know what? This weekend's no good 4me.
DJNelson: What, you're not going 2 another family thing, are you? Y have your parents taken up all your weekends? ☹
Makdiva: Actually, I've kind of been grounded.

That wasn't technically a lie.

'Makeeda!' Delphy yelled into my room.

'What?'

'Mum wants us downstairs.'

DJNelson: What? Why?
Makdiva: Long story. Sorry I have 2 go. Chat soon. X
DJNelson: Fine, but I am going to see you again, right?
Makdiva: Yeah of course! Xx

I went downstairs and walked into the living room. I was nervous. No one had mentioned the whole Tanisha outburst and I knew that it was only a matter of time.

Mum was sitting on the sofa, chatting away in Twi on the phone.

'Hold on. It's Nana-Amma,' she said, handing the receiver over to me.

'Hiya, Nana, *Ghana te sɛn*?' I said brightly.

It was the only new phrase I'd learned. It was basically adjusting the whole 'How are you' thing, to 'How's Ghana?'

'Fine, fine,' she said. 'Well, I know what you've been up to . . .'

'Oh,' I said.

That meant I was about to receive a severe telling off, Nana-style.

'Don't worry, I'm not going to tell you off. You're old enough to know right from wrong and I'm sure your parents will sort everything out.'

Hold on, she was staying out of it? Wow! Nana would usually tell me how disappointed she was at the very least. Once I got the full verbal assault – she was over on a visit and caught me doing something bad when my parents weren't around. After being yelled at in the middle of a shop aged five, I caught on pretty quickly about behaving myself in her company.

'How is your essay going?'

'Fine, I think I know what you mean about Yaa Asantewaa's legacy. Does it have to do with the Golden Stool?' I asked.

'Yes. Well done and don't forget to send me a copy when you've finished it. Take care, Makeeda! Here's Tanisha,' Nana-Amma said.

'Bye, Nana! Hiya, Tanisha!' I said, smiling.

'Ohmigod, Makeeda, what did I do to you?' Tanisha yelled angrily.

'What?' I asked, shocked.

'You implicated me!' Tanisha continued.

'Huh?'

'You told your mum I knew about you and Nelson!' she said.

'Oh yeah,' I said. 'But it's not like anyone will say anything to you . . .'

'Are you crazy? I'm in the middle of Ghana with Nana-Amma! Did you honestly think she'd let this one go?' Tanisha questioned.

She had a point.

'Maybe if you just apologised . . .' I began.

'I'm not the one going out with Nelson! Besides, I've just

spent half an hour apologising to your mum and I have to call your dad tomorrow morning!'

'Well, that's not so bad,' I said.

'That's not my punishment, Makeeda. Girl, that's just pleading for forgiveness!'

'Oh riiiight,' I said, surprised. I really had dropped her in it.

'I swear! I won't see daylight until I start my voluntary work, and that's not till the middle of January. So thanks a lot, Makeeda!' Tanisha said angrily.

'Tanisha, I'm really sorry.'

'Hey, will you two finish up? If the conversation is that important you should buy your own phone cards!' Mum said.

'Bye, Tanisha, and I'm really sorry.'

'OK, Makeeda,' Tanisha said softly and hung up.

'Delphina, get ready for bed, then Makeeda will read to you,' Mum said.

'Yes, Mum,' we both chorused which made us giggle.

Twenty minutes later, Delphy was yelling for me.

I walked into her room. It was slightly smaller than mine and was decorated in blue and pink. The furniture was painted pink and the walls were baby blue, and she had posters of Fairytale on her wardrobe. I noticed a mini biography of Richard Branson beside the latest Malorie Blackman book.

'How come you're reading that?' I said, pointing at the biography.

'I dunno,' she said, shrugging. 'Aren't you going to read to me?'

My parents stopped reading to Delphy nearly five years

ago, because apparently they couldn't get the voices right. So Mum really was punishing me, but I decided to read my essay instead. That way I had the voice thing totally covered.

'Why is it so hot in here?' I asked.

'Because my plant needs the heat,' she said, pointing to a plant pot sitting on her radiator cover. 'It's for my school project.'

'Oh, right,' I said.

'Where's your book?'

'I'm going to read my essay instead.'

'That's not a story!'

'Yes it is. Listen. A long, long time ago . . .'

'It would've been better if you said "once upon a time".'

'Shut up! This isn't a fairytale! What I'm about to tell you really happened,' I said. 'There was a Queen Mother in Asante called Yaa Asantewaa and in 1900 she decided to lead the Asante people to war against the British.'

Delphy yawned.

'Oh thanks,' I said, looking up from my essay.

'Well, get on with it then. Why did she start the war?' she said, snuggling down beneath her duvet.

'Well, when the British came to the Asante kingodom, they wanted to control it.'

'Why?'

'I don't know. I guess they wanted to control its resources, you know, gold, ivory and stuff.'

'Oh.'

'So anyway, in 1896 King Prempeh I and some chiefs held a peaceful *durbar* . . .'

'What's a *durbar*?'

'Look it up, Delphy,' I said, and she gave me a disappointed look. 'Oh OK, it's an official meeting held during colonial times between a British governor and local chief or dignitary.'

'Thanks,' she said, smiling.

'Anyway, they went to discuss British rule of the Asante Kingdom with the Governor, William Maxwell, and within eight days of that meeting, they were all arrested and then exiled in the Seychelles.'

'What! Why?' Delphina questioned, sitting up.

'Stop interrupting me and I'll tell you,' I said, smirking. I was just impressed that I had her attention. Delphy was usually a tough audience.

'Apparently, the British believed that if they removed King Prempeh I they could destroy the Asante Kingdom and seize control of the region.'

'So then what happened?'

'Hold on. Well, as Queen Mother, Yaa Asantewaa automatically became the leader of the Egweso, because its own chief had been sent to exile along with King Prempeh I.'

'And?'

'Delphy! Then the British did something terrible. In 1900, the new governor, Hodgson, demanded to sit on the Golden Stool. I think he knew about Ghanaian folklore surrounding the Golden Stool.'

'What is it?'

'The Golden Stool was the most sacred symbol of the Asantes' strength, independence and spirituality, and there was a link between whoever sat on the stool and the strength of the Asante Kingdom. Hodgson thought that if he sat on the

Golden Stool, he would automatically control the Asantes.'

'Why aren't you asleep?' Dad interrupted, appearing in the doorway.

'Makeeda was telling me about Yaa Asantewaa,' Delphy said.

'Really?' Dad said, impressed.

'Yes – can I stay up? Oh please, Daddy?' Delphina said, putting on her best baby face.

'No. You have school tomorrow and you'll be too tired.'

Wow, he really was becoming resistant to her cute faces.

'Goodnight, Delphina,' he said, kissing her forehead.

'Night, Dad,' she replied sulking.

'Tomorrow,' I said, and I walked back to my room.

Since my argument with Mum, Dad hadn't behaved any different towards me. He told me outright how disappointed he was that I'd lied and with the way I spoke to Mum, but that was it. The atmosphere between Mum and me was still icy, and I hated it. I was beginning to wish that I hadn't said all that stuff about her and Tanisha; at least then I'd only have been punished for going out with Nelson. I missed her. I didn't even have the bits of her I got when Tanisha was around. This was worse. It was like not having a mother at all.

Chapter 14

The Night Before the Assignment Deadline

I was tidying up my essay on my PC when Delphina raced in. She was already in her pyjamas.

'Mum says you have to read to me again.'

'What? Your bedtime isn't for another hour.'

'So? You promised!'

'OK, fine,' I said, reaching for a rough version of my essay. My mobile rang.

'Hey, it's me,' Nelson said.

'Hiya!' I said excitedly, closing my door.

'Wanna meet up outside the library in Harrow?'

'Er . . . when?'

'About forty-five minutes.'

'Um . . .'

'Come on, I haven't seen you in ages!'

'Yeah OK,' I said.

'Later!' he said, and the line went dead.

'Makeeda!' Delphy yelled.

I walked into her room and found her sitting up in anticipation.

'This isn't just a story, is it? It really happened, right?' she asked.

'Yes.'

'OK. You were up to that governor asking to sit on the Golden Stool.'

'Right, well, the Asante dignitaries were totally outraged and Yaa Asantewaa told Hodgson that only the King knew where the Golden Stool was kept, so he should be returned from exile.'

'Wow!' Delphina said, amazed. 'Then what happened?'

'Well, Hodgson refused to return the King and the other chiefs, so Yaa Asantewaa and the other dignitaries left. Eventually Yaa Asantewaa persuaded them that they needed to fight the British. So war was declared.'

'Then what happened?'

'Delphy . . .'

'I know, I know, if I shut up you'll tell me,' Delphy said, making me laugh.

'Hodgson arranged a search party for the Golden Stool, but Yaa Asantewaa's soldiers stopped them and successfully protected it.'

'Good!'

'OK, Delphy,' I said, smiling at her enthusiasm. 'So the war went on until 25th April 1900 when Yaa Asantewaa's troops managed to surround the British base in Kumasi, but in June the governor escaped and alerted the British government and more troops were sent. Eventually Yaa Asantewaa and her troops were captured —'

'Oh no!'

'Yep. She was exiled to the Seychelles and in 1901 the Asante Kingdom became part of the Gold Coast.'

'So she lost the war and was kicked out of the Asante Kingdom?'

'Yes. No. Ohmigod!' I said.

It suddenly dawned on me what Nana-Amma had been talking about when she said I should be thinking about the outcome of Yaa Asantewaa's actions.

'Makeeda, that doesn't make sense,' Delphy said, interrupting my thoughts.

I grabbed a pen from Delphy's desk and scribbled on the last page of my essay.

'What are you doing?'

I told Delphina about my conversation with Nana-Amma.

'So Yaa Asantewaa lost the war, and in 1901 the Asante Kingdom became part of the Britsh empire. But she still managed to protect the Golden Stool,' I said.

'Did she ever return from exile?'

'No, by the time King Prempeh I and his chiefs were returned to the Asante people in 1924, Yaa Asantewaa had already died. She died in 1921.'

'Ohmigod, Makeeda, that's such a sad story,' Delphina said.

'It's not that sad. I mean, she managed to preserve the most significant symbol of Asante identity. If she hadn't done that, maybe we would've lost all our traditions.' I said.

'So she kind of won, right?'

'Yes, Delphy,' I said, gathering my papers. Out of the corner of my eye I saw a ruler sticking out of the plant pot. 'Delphy, what are you growing?'

'Yams.'

'You're growing yams?' I said, trying not to snigger.

'Yeah, but the temperature needs to be between twenty and thirty degrees Celsius for the first eight months of its growth cycle.'

'Eight months? It's really hot in here. Why didn't you just grow broad beans?' I remembered growing a broad bean plant when I was her age that actually grew shoots.

'Too boring. Besides, Aunt Grace said she'd help me.'

I wasn't that surprised. The only plants we had in our house were ones Aunt Grace gave us; she even designed our garden.

'Delphy, you know that it's really unlikely that your plant will grow into a . . .'

'Shut up, Makeeda! My plant doesn't need negative vibes!' Delphina said, getting upset.

'OK, OK, I'm leaving!' I said.

'When I'm a millionaire and everyone's eating my yams, you'll be sorry.'

'Yeah right, Delphy,' I said and left her room.

I looked at my watch. I had twenty-five minutes to convince Mum to let me out and meet up with Nelson. I ran downstairs and had the shortest conversation of my life with my mum. I lied and told her I needed to go to the library to get a book for my essay. She agreed and even asked if I wanted a lift. I said no for obvious reasons and was out of the house and on a bus in record time.

After waiting in front of the library for ten minutes, I decided to move to the bus stop and sent him a text message.

Me: R U running late?

Buses came and went, along with cars that looked too similar to Dad's. I couldn't help but panic that I'd get caught lying again. I kept glancing at my phone and wondered why Nelson hadn't replied to my message, hoping that there had been a weird delay in it reaching his phone.

He was now nearly thirty minutes late and I couldn't help thinking that he'd been in an accident. When I called his mobile, I got his voicemail.

'Hey, where are you? I'm still here, but I can't wait much longer. I'm still grounded,' I said into my phone.

When the fourth bus that Nelson should've been on arrived, I realised that I'd been stood up. Humiliated, I crossed the road and jumped on a bus home.

As the bus pulled into my road I received a text message.

Nelson: Can't make it tonight.
I stared at his reply in disbelief. There was no apology. Was this Nelson's way of dumping me? I cried all the way home.

I walked in to find Mum in exactly the same place I'd left

her, on the couch, reading.

'How was it – did you find anything?' Dad said from the kitchen. He was wearing a T-shirt and jeans and looked a lot cleaner than usual. Mum makes him shower before having dinner, as she hates the smell of the garage.

'Um no, I didn't.'

'Oh right,' he said. I could tell that he'd noticed I'd been crying but, thankfully, he left me alone.

I went to my room and began typing up a new conclusion to my essay.

An hour later Mum joined me.

'Makeeda, I want to talk to you about Tanisha.'

I'd been anticipating this conversation for ages, but it still frightened me. I knew things between us had already changed because of that argument, but this conversation would change things for ever. What if everything between us got worse, rather than better? Worse still, what if nothing changed and I never got my mother back?

I looked at Mum. She looked nervous and I could see what looked like fear in her eyes. The last time I saw that look was a few years ago, when Delphy had trouble breathing and was rushed to hospital. Did Mum feel as anxious as me, or was I imagining it?

I watched as she took a deep breath and continued.

'Makeeda, I need you to . . . to understand how I felt when my sister, your Auntie Jennifer died,' she said. 'I know this will be quite difficult for you to understand but Jenny and I were really close. That's why I was devastated when she died.'

'I remember you wouldn't do anything for weeks,' I said.

For about two weeks after Aunt Jennifer had died, Mum seemed to just shutdown. It was like she wasn't around. Things only got better when Nana-Amma arrived. Within days Mum was almost back to normal, but then the whole Tanisha thing started.

'I ... I know, Makeeda,' she said apologetically. 'It was incredibly difficult for me. All I had left of Jenny were memories, and Tanisha.'

'But that didn't mean you had to leave us out!' I said angrily.

'I know.'

'Why, Mum, why did you do it?' I asked.

'I don't know. Makeeda, I love Tanisha, but you and Delphina are my children – you always come foremost in my heart. You should know that.'

'You never acted like that,' I said. 'You left us out and you're still doing it, Mum!'

It suddenly dawned on me that all I was doing was picking holes in everything she said, but I didn't care. It felt like I was finally telling her everything that Dad had stopped me from saying before.

'You're right,' she said. 'I know I've focussed on Tanisha, but I only did it because I felt that was what Jennifer would have wanted. I was wrong. I know that now,' Mum said quietly.

'OK.'

'I'm just aware that Tanisha still hasn't really come to terms with losing her mother.'

'I know – she never talks about Auntie Jennifer, and gets that funny look in her eyes whenever anyone mentions her,' I said.

'Yes. That's why she still needs our support.'

'OK, but what about me?'

'What do you mean?'

'Mum, you lost your sister and Tanisha lost her mother, but no one remembered that she was also my aunt. Delphy can barely remember her, but I can!' I said, crying. 'I remember that she hated raisins but loved hot-cross buns and always took us swimming.'

Mum stared at me. She was in shock. After a few minutes, she put her arms around me.

'Your dad was right,' she whispered.

'What do you mean?'

'We argued over this. He told me you were hurting, but I dismissed it. I made a mess of things, Makeeda. I'm sorry,' she said as tears welled in her eyes too.

'I'm sorry as well,' I said as she hugged me again.

'What for? You silly thing.'

'The stuff I said.'

'It was from the heart – there's nothing wrong with that,' she said, wiping her eyes and returning to normal. 'So you and Nelson . . .'

'Sorry I lied.'

'Your father and I have decided that you can see him on the following conditions: if your grades slip, it's over, and he can only come here if either your father or I are home.'

'Is that it?' I said, astonished. These rules were pretty simple to keep.

'No, there's more. Family functions always come before your seeing him, plus you can spend six hours with him over the weekend. Don't forget with Christmas coming your Sundays will be for church.'

'Six hours?'

'Yes, you're only fourteen!'

'Nearly fifteen.'

'In nearly seven months, Missy!' Mum said, laughing.

'OK.'

'Oh and nothing but kissing. That is all you're doing?'

'Ohmigod!' I said shaking my head.

'What?' Mum said, barely concealing a look of panic. 'Do we need to have a chat?'

'No!'

Anything but the sex chat. Mum and Dad both had the same conversation with me when I was twelve about periods, and another when I turned fourteen. Totally embarrassing.

'Mum, that's probably the easiest rule to follow,' I said, smiling. I need lots of kissing practice – I'm sure I'm not doing it right. That's if I still have a boyfriend after tonight.

'Good,' Mum said, looking relieved.

'Mum are we going to Ghana for Christmas?' I'd been avoiding this question for ages.

'No, your father and I were simply considering it.'

As I watched her leave, I suddenly realised that I didn't know when my grounding ended.

'Mum, when does my grounding finish?'

'Sunday,' she said, smiling.

I spent the rest of the night re-reading my essay until about eleven p.m. when Dad told me to just print it out and get some sleep. I couldn't help it. It had to be good, especially as Mrs

Hipman hadn't actually given me permission to write it. I lay in my bed thinking over my conversation with Mum. Even though everything had been said, I still wasn't convinced that things would be OK between us. I was happy that the atmosphere had gone but, because everything had been so weird for so long, deep down I knew there were no guarantees until Tanisha was in England again. That would be the real test. Thinking about it made me nervous. But it still didn't stop me thinking about Nelson. He knew I was still grounded. He knew I had taken a risk to see him. Why didn't he show up?

Chapter 15

Sticks and Stones

'Makeeda, you will have to come into school next week,' Mrs Hipman said.

It was just the two of us in the classroom, as everyone else had rushed off to their next lesson.

'What! Why?' I asked.

We were in the final week of school before the Christmas holidays. The last thing I wanted to do was to come in next week! I still had shopping to do.

'For a start, I was quite clear when I told you not to write this essay!' she said angrily.

I winced. Mrs Hipman was one of those teachers who rarely shouted in class, so when she did you knew you were in serious trouble.

'I have a good mind not to mark this,' she said, waving my essay in the air.

'Oh, Miss,' I whined. 'I spent ages on it. You were right – it was a nightmare finding the books,' I added.

She peered at me over her glasses. I tried to give her a desperate look, like the one Delphy gives Dad. There was no way I was going to redo that assignment, so I had to try everything I knew.

'OK, Makeeda,' she said with a sigh.

'Really, Miss? You'll mark it?'

'Yes, but I'm warning you, if you ever try a stunt like this again, you'll be in front of the headmistress so fast your feet won't touch the ground. Is that clear?'

'Yes, Miss.'

'Right, well I'll see you here next week, around half past two and I'll decide then if you have to rewrite this assignment.'

'Yes, Miss, and thanks,' I said, leaving the room as her next class rushed in.

I was so glad Mrs Hipman was going to mark it that I wasn't bothered about having to come in next week.

I saw Mel and Laura standing outside our next classroom. We'e not allowed to enter unless a teacher is present.

'Hey.'

'Hey, so are you all sorted for Christmas then?' Mel asked.

'Nope, you know my mum doesn't allow anyone to mention it until the second week in December,' I said.

'Huh?' Laura said.

'My mum places an emphasis on the birth of Christ as opposed to Santa Claus and Rudolph.'

'Seriously?' Laura said, horrified.

'Yeah, the decorations in our house have more to do with Jesus than Father Christmas, apart from the tree.'

'Wow!' Laura said.

Mel and I just laughed at her reaction. It was the same every time I explained it to people.

'How's Nelson?' Mel asked.

'Um, I think he's OK. I haven't seen him in a while.'

Our drama teacher came rushing towards us.

'Sorry I'm late, ladies. Let's get started,' he said, opening the studio door.

Halfway through the lesson, Bharti appeared, handing a note over to our teacher. I wanted to find out where she'd been, but she was put in the same workshop as Laura so I had to wait.

When the final bell rang, I ran after Bharti.

'Bharti! Wait up! Can I walk to the bus stop with you?' I asked.

'OK,' she said, shrugging.

'Guess what?' I said.

'What?'

'Nelson stood me up,' I said.

'Nelson?' Bharti questioned.

'Yeah, and my parents have agreed to let me go out with him. Which is really great and stuff, but I'm —' I began.

'Makeeda!' Bharti interrupted. 'I'm not being funny or anything, but all you ever seem to talk about now is Nelson.'

'No I don't,' I said.

'Yes, you do. You never once ask me about my life; it's always about yours.'

'That's not true.'

'This is the reason you forgot to meet me a few weeks back.'

'I . . . I just forgot. It was an accident, Bharti!'

'You're totally obsessed with having a boyfriend and being someone's girlfriend, because it makes you more like them,' she said, glancing at Mel and Laura. 'Popular!' she spat at me.

'That's not true!' I said.

It was true that going out with Nelson had meant that more girls in my school and guys from his said hello to me, but I really did like Nelson too. That was why I was going out with him. It wasn't to be popular.

'Are you sure, Makeeda?' Bharti said, giving me an incredulous look.

'You're just jealous!' I shouted. 'You wish you had a boyfriend and can't handle it that I've got Nelson!'

By this time I was standing head to head with Bharti. I could feel my anger slowly rising throughout our conversation, and it felt that nothing but hitting her would really make me feel any better. By the look on her face, I guess she felt exactly the same way about me.

'What? Only someone as self-centred as you would think that!' Bharti screamed back.

Mel rushed to stand between us.

'Come on, you two!' she said, using one hand to push Bharti away from me and her body to push me backwards.

'Now that's what I call friendship,' Laura said, smirking.

'Shut up, Laura!' Bharti, Mel and I chorused together.

'Whoa, it was just an observation,' Laura said.

Bharti stepped away from us.

'Makeeda, you can come to the shops with us. We're meeting Jordan and Stephen. Nelson might be there,' Mel said.

'Oh great,' Laura said.

Mel flashed her 'don't go there' look and I was too furious to respond to her.

A bus pulled up and Bharti headed straight for it.

'Bye Mel, Laura,' she said. The doors closed and I watched the girl formerly known as my best friend head home.

'Well?' Mel said.

'Yeah, I'll come,' I said, calming down.

'I see you sorted things out with Bharti,' Mel said, smiling.

'Well, I thought I had,' I replied.

I was still in a state of shock. Why had Bharti and I come so close to fighting?

Mel, Laura and I walked in the direction of the shops. Initially Mel kept trying to reassure me that Bharti didn't mean what she said and within two days we'd make up over cups of hot chocolate. I wasn't convinced, because I knew Bharti meant everything she said and, the worse thing was, so did I. I was so furious with her; I needed her, but she threw it back in my face. Who else could I talk to about Nelson, Mum, everything? Mel and Laura had become so close that I barely got a look in, and I got the impression that Mel fancied Jordan and was using me to get to him. Once she realised I wasn't in the chatty mood, she and Laura began discussing their next netball match.

'Hey, Makeeda!' Nelson said, walking towards me with a grin plastered on his face.

In the distance I could see Stephen and Jordan having another one of their heated debates. I waved to them and watched as Laura and Mel joined their conversation. The closer Nelson got to me the more confused I felt. He was smiling at me, but I wanted to scream at him for not showing up last night. As he hugged me the words never left my lips. I'd missed him so much I didn't want to ruin things.

'All right?' he said.

'Yeah fine,' I lied.

We pulled apart and held hands, until we reached the others.

'Shut up! You can't buy a computer game for your mum!' Stephen was saying to Jordan.

'What's going on?' Nelson said.

'You won't believe what Jordan wants to get his mum for Christmas . . . a computer game!' Stephen said.

'Huh?' I said in disbelief, as Mel and Laura laughed.

'Hold it,' Jordan said. 'My mum could be, like, a PlayStation genius . . .'

'Is she?' Laura asked.

'Well . . .' Jordan said.

'Just admit it! It's for you,' said Stephen.

'Well . . .' Jordan said again.

'It's pretty lame, mate!' Nelson added.

'OK then, what have you got yours?' Jordan asked.

I looked over at Stephen, who looked ready to throttle Jordan. I guess only Stephen and I knew about Nelson's strained relationship with his mother.

Nelson's face momentarily fell, but he recovered and mumbled, 'Oh, vouchers.'

'Oh, right,' Jordan said.

'You OK?' I whispered to Nelson.

'Yeah,' he said, releasing his hand from my grip. I watched as he began fiddling with his laces.

'I could help you find something for her, if you want?' Mel said, turning to Jordan.

I bet she could. Mel rarely volunteers for anything that doesn't involve sports. I guess tonsil tennis counts.

'Aren't you meeting Jason later?' Laura asked.

'No, not today,' Mel replied, giving Laura a fierce look.

As I watched Mel and Laura, I wondered if they were both interested in Jordan.

'Makeeda? Makeeda!' Mel said angrily.

'What?' I said, more guiltily than I would have liked.

'You're always somewhere else! Come on,' Mel said, pushing me.

I hadn't noticed that the others were heading into a café. I wondered why Nelson had gone ahead without waiting for me.

We sat down in the corner of the café before ordering. Stephen decided to shout Jordan a drink because he was going to need his money for his mum's present, whilst Laura had her usual bottle of mineral water as she only drank one brand. I watched as Nelson went to get a cappuccino without offering to get me a drink. It only dawned on him when Jordan asked him if he'd forgotten someone. I quickly replied that I didn't want anything, but Nelson didn't seem that bothered either way.

'So, who's your best kiss ever?' Laura said, when he came back.

'This girl, I mean woman, in my nan's shop last summer,' Jordan replied. 'She was two pence short and asked if she could make it up with a kiss.'

'I don't think so, mate. Laura said the *best* kiss ever. Not *fantasy* kiss,' Stephen said.

'Ooohh, that was harsh!' Nelson said, making us laugh.

'It happened; I've got it on CCTV!'

'That's got to be illegal,' Laura commented.

'Yeah, I bet you keep tapes of all the good-looking women who come into your store,' Stephen said, shaking his head. 'Nasty boy!'

'Nah, that's just sad. I'm not sad!' Jordan said.

We all went quiet.

'I'm not!' Jordan protested.

'No, of course not,' Mel said, shifting away from him in her seat.

'Hey!' Jordan said, gently hitting her shoulder.

I saw a smile leap across Mel's face. I guessed Jason was officially history now.

'What about you, Nelson?' Laura asked.

'Hey, that's not fair. His girlfriend's sitting next to him!' Stephen said.

'Oh come on, what's the big deal? Makeeda doesn't mind if he mentions an ex, do you?' Laura asked.

'No,' I replied.

Sometimes Laura made it too difficult to actually like her. Bharti would have loved this. She'd be laughing and I wouldn't mind, because we'd still be mates, so I'd be laughing too. I was rubbish! We'd only just had a huge argument and I already missed her.

'I'm not sure,' Nelson said.

'Cop out!' Laura said.

'Shut up, Laura!' Stephen said. I got the impression that he didn't like Laura very much.

'Hold up, I was going to say that I don't think I can judge my best kiss ever till I've experienced other kisses,' Nelson continued.

'I see where you're going!' Jordan said, winking heavily.

Ohmigod! What the hell does that mean? I know what it means! Why is he telling them this? Why is telling me about his next girlfriend?

'No, Jordan!' Nelson said. 'I just meant that it might not have happened yet.' I noticed that he avoided eye contact with me.

I was speechless. I couldn't believe what he had just said. Out of the corner of my eye, I could see the look of surprise on Laura's face and Stephen's eyes suddenly hitting the floor. Mel was too busy chatting to someone on her phone to notice the almost eerie silence that followed Nelson last response. It was as if they all knew I was about to become Nelson's ex.

'What about you, Laura?' Jordan asked.

'Yeah, you're so busy asking all the questions, spill!' Stephen said accusingly.

My phone beeped.

Nick: I hate shopping it's a nightmare!

I was too distracted to reply.

'Easy, last summer, Greece, sunrise, with a local . . .'

'A holiday romance?' Stephen said mockingly.

'He was a local DJ and twenty . . .'

'Yeah, sure,' Stephen said. 'Why would a twenty-year-old go out with a fourteen-year-old?'

'Whatever!' Laura replied, flicking her hair.

'I have to go,' I said.

'Really?' Stephen said, clearly disappointed.

I wished Nelson felt that way, but for some reason he seemed more preoccupied with showing Jordan a text message.

'Yeah, I forgot to pick up my mum's dry cleaning and they close at six-thirty,' I lied.

'Oh right, well, see you around,' Stephen said, smiling.

'Yeah, later Makeeda,' said Jordan.

Jordan dug Nelson in the ribs before he looked up from his phone.

'Oh right, bye!' Nelson said.

I saw Stephen and Jordan give Nelson a puzzled look, whilst Laura just kept looking from him to me.

'You're going?' Mel asked. She'd only just finished her phone call and once again had missed everything. 'You OK?' she asked.

'Yeah,' I lied.

'OK, I'll call you later, or something,' she said, hugging me.

I tried desperately not to cry.

'Bye!' I said, hastily grabbing my coat and bag. The distance to the café doors felt over a mile long. I knew it would be too obvious if I started running out, so I tried to keep my feet moving at a moderate pace until the door closed behind me. Then I ran. By then, the tears had started and didn't want to stop.

'Makeeda, Makeeda?' Nick said, grabbing my shoulders.

I turned around to see him carrying several bags of shopping including a bright red and green tube of wrapping paper.

'I've been yelling for ages! What's wrong?' he said, on noticing my tears.

I told him everything and he made the same face he had when he took on José Santos.

'No, Nick. I don't need you to sort him out!'

'I wasn't going to. You're old enough to do this one on your own,' Nick said.

I actually wasn't expecting that from him. In fact, that was the shortest lecture he had ever given me.

'Whatever,' I said, attempting to sound indifferent.

'He's messing you around, Makeeda, and I can't work out why you're allowing him to get away with it,' Nick said.

'I'm not!' I said defensively.

'Really? Well, it's up to you but, if you can make a big deal out of doing that essay on Yaa Asantewaa, then I can't see why you can't make your boyfriend be straight with you.'

He had a point, as usual.

'You're not exactly making me feel better,' I said.

'No, but you can have this,' he said, giving me half of his chocolate bar.

'Oh thanks,' I said sarcastically, and he immediately withdrew it from my hand. 'I'm kidding,' I added.

'Better be,' he replied, handing it back.

'Listen, I've still got to find something for my gran or I'd sit here with you.'

'No you wouldn't, you'd say you had a ton of revision to do and disappear!'

'OK, I wouldn't, but I'd consider it, because that's what family does. Considers stuff,' he said, smiling.

'Thanks,' I said.

'Oh yeah!' Nick said, pulling my hair. 'You've got to sort out this apocalyptic feud you have with Bharti – it's getting pretty pathetic.'

'Ouch!' I said.

'You deserved that one. It is definitely girly stuff and this time I'm staying well clear of it!'

'I didn't ask you to . . .'

'I know, and I'm not offering again,' he said, standing up and adjusting his bags. 'See ya around, cuz,' he added, before disappearing into the growing mass of commuters and late night Christmas shoppers.

I caught my bus home and really thought about what he'd said. I didn't understand why Nelson was being so mean to me, but I knew I'd had enough of it. There was no way I was going to let him get away with treating me like that. Nick was right. I'd faced Mum and Mrs Hipman, so why couldn't I face Nelson? Was I that afraid of us splitting up?

Chapter 16

Plantain Wars

It was two days into the Christmas holidays and I had successfully crammed all my Christmas shopping into the space of three hours, under one roof: Brent Cross Shopping Centre. I walked into the house to the sound of raised voices and saw Mum chasing Delphina upstairs.

'What's going on, Dad?'

'Your sister got caught selling sweets at school,' he said, heading into the kitchen.

'Really?'

'Yes, she managed to undercut the tuck shop and take away their business.'

I laughed. I couldn't help it.

'Makeeda, this isn't funny. If she gets suspended, it could damage her high school chances. We only found out today because they sent us a letter,' Dad said, smirking.

'Come on, Dad, you're proud of her, aren't you?'

'Makeeda, what she did was wrong and that's all there is to it. However, her profits nearly doubled and she even managed to include healthy alternatives,' Dad said.

'Wow! I'm impressed,' I told him.

No one was sure how Delphina had acquired her business acumen, but it worked. Earlier this year she told Dad he could make money teaching people basic car maintenance as well as servicing their cars. Dad tried it out for a month and it's become a steady earner.

'She said she built it up from a bag of lollipops. Do you know anything about it?'

My face dropped. Ohmigod, if Delphy implicated me, Mum and Dad wouldn't let me see daylight. I was going to kill her. No wonder she had more money for Mum and Dad's presents this year.

'Lollipops? No,' I said, reaching for an apple. If there was food in my mouth, I was less likely to incriminate myself.

'Haven't you got that meeting today?'

'Yeah,' I said, gulping down a huge piece of apple. 'I'll leave just after I've hidden my presents,' I said.

'So what is it this year – Arsenal away kit, maybe?'

'Dad!'

'What? It was a simple question? . . .'

'You don't give us enough pocket money for that!' I added.

'Cheeky!' Dad said, smiling. 'Mum and I won't be in later, so you need to come home and look after your sister as soon as you've finished at school.'

'OK,' I replied.

'Makeeda, you can have anyone round except Nelson, as we won't be in.'

'Yeah, OK.'

Considering I hadn't spoken to him in nearly a week, that rule was easy to follow.

I rushed upstairs and hid all the presents and then caught the bus to school.

It was really weird walking through my school during the holidays. The caretaker let me in and told me to go to the history department. I walked along the empty corridors and kept expecting to hear the loudness of a bunch of girls screaming with laughter or rushing to their next class, but it never happened. It felt eerie.

The first thing Mrs Hipman did was tell me again how disappointed she was that I'd disobeyed her. I knew then that I'd failed the assignment. It wasn't until she shoved my essay in front of me that I tuned into her. I stared at the grade and then looked up to see her grinning back at me.

'Ohmigod, I got an A?' I said, shocked.

'Makeeda, I'm so proud of you!'

'I got an A?'

'Yes, Makeeda, and if you work hard towards your exams you could achieve an A* at GCSE.'

'I got an A!' I said, smiling. 'No offence, but they're like gold dust in your class, Miss!'

She laughed.

It was true. Bharti and I once calculated that Mrs Hipman gave out about eight grade As per academic year!

'Yes, Makeeda. Like I always say, it only takes hard work and commitment and you've shown that. I didn't want you to write this essay, because I believed that it would be too difficult to get the resources and that kind of patience normally comes with age. What you've written, however, is a thought-provoking essay that you've managed to relate to the use of traditions by modern-day Ghanaians. I don't think you realise what you've achieved here, do you?'

'Well . . .'

I actually liked Mrs Hipman even though she was strict. She was different to some of the other teachers; she really believed that everyone could achieve anything they wanted. Bharti and I used to say it was a shame she brought hard work into the equation, but no teacher was perfect.

'Makeeda, this essay crosses into sociology. It was a fascinating read!'

'Um, thanks, Miss,' I said, interrupting her.

Thank God I wrote that last paragraph, about the legacy of tradition and identity that Yaa Asantewaa had instilled in modern-day Ghanaians through protecting the Golden Stool. I knew I had Nana-Amma to thank for that.

'Did you enjoy writing it?'

'Yes, Miss,' I said. 'It was difficult in places, but I was glad I was able to write it.'

'Well, on this occasion I'm glad you completely ignored me, but don't do it again.'

'No promises, Miss!' I said, giving her a grin.

'Makeeda!' she said, laughing. 'Wish your family a Merry Christmas from me.'

'I will. Thanks again!' I said as I ran out of the school.

An A? I was still in shock. I decided to send a few text messages, to everyone but Bharti and Nelson.

Me: I got an A!
Mel: Well done, don't suppose she told you what I got?
Me: No.
Mel: Bet u didn't even ask!

Mel knew me well.

Me: Wanna come round for a bit?
Mel: Yeah, I can give you your present.
Me: OK, I'll be home in 30mins.

As I sat on the bus home, my mind kept drifting between Nelson and Bharti. I missed Bharti and felt angry at Nelson. He didn't seem bothered by anything that had happened. Maybe I was right. Maybe he was just working his way up to dumping me.

Mel: W R U?
Me: R U @ my house? I'm just walking up the high road.
Mel: Meet me at the bus stop ASAP.
Me: Y? OK.

That was weird. Mel knew the way to my house. As I headed back to the bus stop, I saw an old woman sitting down next to a girl wrapped up in a purple coat and black boots; she couldn't see me, as her hair covered the book she was reading. It was

Bharti. I could tell by the way she shoved her face right into the spine of the book. Then, suddenly, she looked up and saw me. I froze on the spot.

'Excuse me, love,' the old woman said prodding me with her walking stick. 'You're blocking my view! I can't see if the bus is coming if you stand there!'

'Oh, sorry,' I said.

I looked over at Bharti, who was laughing, but as we weren't talking it was awkward. I mean, was she laughing at me in a spiteful way? Or laughing at me in a friendly way?

I moved to stand in front of her.

'Have you seen Mel?' I asked neutrally.

'No, I'm waiting for her too,' she replied. She picked up her book and began reading again.

Great! She obviously still hates me, I thought.

Bharti's phone beeped, then so did mine.

Mel: I'M NOT COMING SO SORT IT OUT!

'Ohmigod, I'm going to kill her!' Bharti and I screamed simultaneously.

The old woman narrowed her eyes and gave us a wary look. With one hand she clutched her bag to her chest, whilst the other took a firm grip on her walking stick.

Bharti and I exchanged looks, then laughed. I sat down beside her away from the old woman.

'I love your coat,' I said.

'Thanks, it's a present from Tejas.'

'Really?'

171

'Yeah, he reckons I should dress more like a lady. Hitesh's girlfriend helped him pick it out.'

'Oh right,' I said. 'You know you look really different.'

'Yeah?'

'Definitely. You've got a different vibe to you now.'

'Well ... I'm eating properly and I've been getting more toned since I started doing those street dance classes at the gym.'

'Wow! That's really good,' I said, impressed.

'It's better than all those rubbish diets I was doing and I feel different too,' said Bharti.

'Good,' I said, smiling.

'Yeah, and I'm over Hitesh. His girlfriend is really nice but, from what she told me, he's a bit of a nightmare.'

'How?'

'He forgets important stuff like birthdays.'

'Oh,' I said.

If there was one thing that bugged Bharti, it was people who forgot birthdays. For her there was never a decent excuse.

'Exactly,' she said.

An awkward silence blanketed us. I didn't want Bharti to stop speaking to me; it felt like old times with her talking about Hitesh, and it made me realise how much I'd missed her. I kept thinking of things to say, when the old lady used her walking stick to move another commuter out of her way.

'Ohmigod, she's at it again!' I whispered.

'I know! Haven't you noticed that all three buses have been but she hasn't boarded one?' said Bharti.

'Yeah, but neither have we.'

'Good point.'

'Do you want to come to my place?' I asked.

I watched as her face flickered with some kind of unpleasant memory. I was really scared she'd say no – after all, we still hadn't sorted things out.

'Yeah, OK.'

We walked in silence for a bit, dodging the passers by with huge shopping bags bursting with Christmas stuff.

'Makeeda?' Bharti said. 'How did it go with your essay?'

'I got an A,' I muttered.

'Really? That's brilliant!' Bharti said, genuinely pleased for me.

'Thanks.'

I thought it would be as good a time as any to say sorry. I knew that I hadn't had much luck with apologies in the past, but I hoped it wouldn't be such a problem now.

'Bharti?'

'Makeeda, I'm really sorry!' she blurted out suddenly.

'Oh!' I said, shocked.

'Listen, I know that I've been really mean to you, especially when you apologised and . . .'

'Um . . . hold up!' I said but she ignored me.

'I just want to say that, when I said that you were obsessed with Nelson, I didn't mean it. I was overreacting.'

'OK, and I didn't mean to call you jealous. Especially as I was absolutely no help with Hitesh.'

'Mates?'

'Yeah,' I replied, hugging her.

'At last!' Mel said.

She was standing at my front door in a bright blue puffa

jacket, pale blue scarf and dark red cord trousers. And she was jumping up and down.

'What's with the jumping?' I asked.

'Joke, right? I'm cold, Makeeda! I've been standing here for nearly an hour!' Mel said.

Bharti and I exchanged surprised looks. We knew she couldn't have been there for more than twenty minutes tops.

'Delphy's in,' I said, unlocking the door.

'Whaaat?' Mel screamed in my ear. 'I knocked!'

'Oh yeah, she's not allowed to answer the door unless someone else is in,' I explained.

We walked in to find Delphina piling more decorations on to the Christmas tree. It looked like it was going to topple over with the additional weight, but I didn't say anything to her. She was doing it to annoy Mum and Dad.

'Hey, did you hear about the kid at Delphy's school who was outselling the tuck shop?' Mel asked, as I handed around biscuits and drinks.

'Yeah, my little cousin said it looks like the money they made will go to charity, probably Oxfam,' Bharti added.

Ohmigod, people know? I'd better warn Mum.

'Didn't you know about it?' Mel asked.

'Um . . . well, yeah, I heard about it,' I replied.

'You know, when I heard, I thought it was something Delphy would do. Mad, huh?' Bharti said, laughing.

'Yeah, me too,' said Mel, joining in.

I gave a hollow laugh and took a sip of my drink.

Luckily Mum and Aunt Grace walked in with bags of food, so they both dropped the subject. When Mum asked us to fry some plantain, I expected Bharti and Mel to come up with an excuse, but they didn't. We were relegated to the kitchen, while Mum and Aunt Grace caught up on the latest Ghanaian film.

As I carefully finished pouring the oil into the frying pan, Mel had almost finished slicing the plantains. Bharti had finished her peeling duties and was busy wrapping the skins in a newspaper for recycling.

'Can I put them in?' Mel asked.

'Yeah,' I said, giving her some room. I watched as pieces of plantain fell into the hot oil and immediately began sizzling.

'I'm not turning them over though,' Mel said, standing back.

'Chicken!' I replied.

'This is a new top,' she said, looking down at a sweater I'd seen more than ten times this month alone.

'Yeah, whatever!' I said, checking the plantain.

'You know, my star sign said I was going to have a major disagreement twice,' said Bharti.

'Yeah?' I said.

'Uh huh. It said something about this huge disagreement paving the way for a new and better existence. Weird thing is yours said something similar. We were fated to argue, Makeeda.'

Mel and I exchanged looks.

'Was it written in the stars then?' Mel asked, sniggering.

'Yeah. I reckon it was,' Bharti said seriously, making Mel and I burst into laughter.

'What? It's true!' Bharti said.

'Hey, Laura told me what happened with Nelson,' Mel said suddenly.

It completely killed my vibe. I tried to ignore her and started flipping the plantain over gently.

'What happened?' Bharti asked.

Mel told her everything Laura had said about the café, and surprisingly it didn't have the usual overtones of 'I hate Makeeda' all over it. I heard Bharti gasp in shock, and knew they were waiting for me to speak.

'Makeeda?' Bharti said.

'Hold on, I'm taking the plantain out,' I said, carefully spooning the slices into a sieve.

I really didn't want to talk about Nelson. I'd spent nearly a week not thinking about him, or at least attempting it. I had to face facts. He wasn't interested in me any more and was going to make it official any day now. When I told Mel and Bharti, they had puzzled looks on their faces. Mel said, if I was right, she would have heard about it from one of his friends. She meant Jordan. The only problem with that was that I knew that Stephen and Hakeem were closer to Nelson than Jordan. Bharti then asked if we'd had an argument, or if Nelson had any reason to be upset with me, but I told her no, as I hadn't told him about being forbidden to see him or that my parents never knew about him. That was when Mel pulled her uh-oh face.

'You didn't!' I said.

'You said you'd tell him,' she said defensively.

'What's going on?' Bharti asked.

Before we could explain, Mum walked in and swiped the plate of plantain.

'I hope you girls aren't sitting here eating it all,' Mum said.

'We haven't even sampled our handiwork yet, Auntie,' Mel

said, attempting to grab a slice, but Mum ducked out of the way.

'A likely story, Melanie,' Mum replied.

I saw Mel wince at her full name being used.

'Oh, I nearly forgot, Makeeda, we're going to your Auntie Anita's place on the twenty-sixth for dinner,' Mum informed me, reaching for some forks and side plates.

Another family gathering – whoopee do dah!

'So?' Bharti asked, as soon as Mum was out of earshot.

'Mel told Nelson I was forbidden to see him.'

'Ohmigod!' Bharti said.

'It wasn't like that!' Mel protested. 'I just said how great it was that Makeeda's parents changed their mind. How could I know that he didn't know? The boy even smiled at me!'

'Weird,' Bharti said.

'I'm so glad Laura told me what happened,' Mel said.

'Hold on, why didn't he just ask you what was going on?' Bharti said to me.

'Exactly. Instead he just humiliated me twice!' I said angrily.

I saw Mel and Bharti exchange worried glances. I didn't want their sympathy I just wanted to throttle Nelson for being so horrible to me. Even if he knew about me keeping him a secret, it didn't excuse his behaviour.

I started piling more plantain into the frying pan. My mobile rang and Bharti answered it. I heard the surprise in her voice.

'Makeeda, you're not going to believe it.'

I looked at her like she was crazy. Then I saw the name on my phone. Nelson.

'Calm down,' said Mel, taking the spoon from my hand.

'OK,' I said to Mel. 'Yeah?' I said into my phone.

I decided to walk into the corner. I stared out on to the garden and saw Delphy's football in the distance covered in silver-tipped grass leaves. Our garden never seemed to fully thaw in winter.

'Makeeda? Makeeda?'

'Yeah.'

'I ... I ... wanted to apologise for standing you up,' he said. His voice didn't seem as confident as it usually was.

'Why are you telling me this now? It happened ages ago and I've seen you since. Remember?' I said angrily.

I saw Bharti and Mel exchange looks of shock at my outburst.

'Makeeda, I'm calling to ...'

'Listen, if you're calling to dump me because I'm obviously never going to be "your best kiss ever", then fine. Take the easy route and do it over the phone, because if I see you ...'

'Hold on a minute!' Nelson interrupted. 'I never said I was going to dump you! That's not why I'm calling.'

'It's not?' I said, shocked.

'No. I'm calling because I want to sort this out! Another thing: don't play the victim. You never told me that your parents didn't know I was your boyfriend, or the real reason you were grounded, Mel did!' he said angrily.

'Yeah, but that didn't give you the right to treat me the way you did!'

'No, but how do you think I felt, Makeeda? I went to your house and met your mum. The woman must have been in shock when I turned up!'

I laughed. It was weird, but I could imagine the look on Mum's face.

'It's not funny!' Nelson said, but he couldn't help himself either and started laughing too. 'Listen, Makeeda, can't we sort this out?' he said softly.

'Yeah, OK.' I said.

'Can we meet up today?'

'No. I won't be free till the twenty-seventh.'

'The twenty-seventh? OK. How about two o'clock, Brent Cross Shopping Centre?

'Fine,' I said, and he hung up.

'Well?' Mel said.

'He apologised and we're meeting up on the twenty-seventh.'

'What?' Bharti said astonished.

'Oh, sorry, I forgot about going shopping,' I confessed. Bharti and I usually met up on the twenty-seventh to go sales shopping with our Christmas money.

'I'll go with you,' Mel volunteered.

'No thanks. If I wanted to spend hours looking at sports gear, I'd sit in the local gym,' Bharti said to Mel.

'Ouch!' Mel said, shocked.

I laughed. Mel had a habit of being mesmerised by the latest gadgets and products in a sports shop, even when we were looking for decent heels (or flats in my case). She once spent the money her mum gave her for a dress on a special tracksuit that had fabric that used your sweat to help cool your body down. Bharti and I couldn't see the point in it but then Mel was the one who woke up at six a.m. to go running and did Taekwondo twice a week.

'Do you want to swap rooms? We're about to sort out dinner,' Mum said, smiling.

'OK,' I said, taking a huge plate of plantain with us to the living room. 'That's the last batch in there,' I said, pointing to the frying pan full of plantain.

'OK,' Mum said.

'Eh, you girls are growing so fast!' Aunt Grace said, smiling as she walked past us.

We flopped down on to the sofa and turned a music channel on. The front door bell rang and I heard Mum saying hello to Nick.

A few minutes later, Nick walked in with a plate of hot plantain, biscuits and a drink.

'All right?' he said, sitting down. 'I left your present under the tree,' he said to me.

'Cheers, did you find yours?'

'Yeah.'

Every year we just left each other's presents under the tree.

I exchanged brief looks with Bharti and Mel. We were all thinking the same thing.

'Need any help with that?' Bharti asked Nick, as she eyed his food.

'Yeah, it looks too much for one,' I added, before all three of us began attacking him for the hot plantain and biscuits.

'Hey!' he said, trying to save his food. In the end he coughed on the plantain and we all backed off.

'That's nasty, man!' Mel said.

'You'd know.'

'Don't start, you two!' Bharti said.

We sat there watching the music videos for half an hour before it suddenly dawned on me that I hadn't bought a present for Nelson.

'You've only got a few hours left,' said Bharti.

'Why didn't you buy it earlier?' Nick asked.

Bharti told him about my conversation with Nelson, and I saw Nick visibly flinch but tried to ignore his reaction. Mel caught a look of annoyance he gave me.

'Not jealous again, are we?' she said quietly.

'Shut up, Mel!' Nick told her. His face had gone red.

'Ohmigod, can you two leave me out of it?' I pleaded.

'He's a jerk!' Mel said, grabbing her coat.

'Yeah and you're a cow,' Nick said angrily.

'Great, like MSN messaging wasn't bad enough,' Bharti commented, buttoning up her coat.

Within minutes of us leaving my house, Bharti managed to solve the source of the Nick/Mel feud: Nick's failure to turn up at Mel's birthday party. We stood in my street as she told Mel to get over herself and Nick that he should have told Mel himself that he couldn't go to her party, and she made them apologise to each other. But I saw a look in Nick's eyes that meant he wasn't going to forgive Mel that quickly. And I had a weird feeling that he didn't approve of me buying Nelson a Christmas present. He didn't come with us as he had to see his grandmother but, as I watched him running for his bus, it suddenly hit me: whatever I did, I seemed to upset somebody.

At least Nelson and I were a few steps closer to sorting things out. But how long would that last?

Chapter 17

Xmas MSN Message

I was chilling on the couch after our huge Christmas meal, when I remembered that I was meant to be chatting to Tanisha online. I looked across at Mum, who was caressing a sleepy Delphina's hair as she lay across her lap, and Dad, who had just returned from dropping off Aunt Grace. He was wearing the Arsenal kit Mum had bought him and the scarf from Delphy and me that hadn't left his neck since we gave it to him. Mum only stopped playing the *1980s Greatest Hits* album Dad gave her when Delphy and I complained of headaches.

I jumped up and made my way through all the wrapping paper still strewn across the floor (Mum and Dad never made us tidy up straight away), and headed off to my room. I was carrying an mp3 player, make-up from Tanisha (that Mum told me I couldn't wear all the time) and envelopes with vouchers.

'Where are you off to?' Dad asked.

'I'm meant to be chatting to Tanisha online.'

'Oh OK, say hello from us,' he said.

Within minutes of switching on my computer an MSN box opened up.

HotT: Maaan Makeeda, ur timekeeping is soooooo wrong!

Makdiva: Happy Christmas 2 u too!

HotT: Well, how is everyone?

Makdiva: Er OK. Except Aunt Grace made me get changed this morning.

HotT: Y?

Makdiva: I was wearing jeans and a T-shirt and apparently u have to wear new or smart clothes because it's Christmas day.

HotT: SHAAAAAME! LOL!

Makdiva: I noticed her giving Dad funny looks for wearing his Arsenal kit after trying it on, but he reminded her it was new.

HotT: LOL! What about Delphy?

Makdiva: The traitor was already wearing her newest ntoma plus a duku, courtesy of Aunt Grace. Conspiracy or what?

HotT: So did your Mum wear out that CD your Dad was giving her?

Makdiva: U should've heard her singing along. Eighties

music is seriously squeaky.

HotT: LOL! I heard about Delphy and the sweetshop.

Makdiva: OMG, has it reached Ghana already?

HotT: Yeah!

This was it; Delphy's name, not to mention my family's, would be dirt. No one ever gets kicked out of primary school – well as far as I knew Ghanaian kids didn't. The fact that Delphy was seriously close to it was bad enough.

HotT: Anyway, Nana's going to talk to her later. She's a bit worried about having delinquent grandkids, which is totally OTT cos I'm OK. ☺ So how did the whole Delphy's Dodgy Deals Inc get started anyway?

Makdiva: Your lollipops!

HotT: What r u talking about?

Makdiva: U gave me that bag of lollipops; I gave them to Delphy, and she sold them to her school mates and made ££.

I stopped typing as I could see that Tanisha was typing at the same time.

HotT: OMG! SHUT UP! U R LYING!

Makdiva: No UR IN IT UP 2 UR NECK! So far, Delphy's keeping up the code of silence. ☺

HotT: Nice 2 know one of u has. ☺

She had a point but I wasn't going to take the bait. Mum and I had sorted things out.

HotT: Why did u give them 2 her?

Makdiva: Why not? I didn't think she'd set up a flaming business with them.

HotT: It's impressive though.

Makdiva: U reckon? I had to deny everything to Mel and Bharti.

HotT: Yeah, that's what u do 4 family! I hope she doesn't grass on us. U got me punishment on the poultry farm next door for two days, plus babysitting some random cousin's brats!

Makdiva: LOL! What was the farm like?

HotT: I'm becoming vegetarian! They made me pluck feathers off the chickens using boiling water and my bare hands!! That smell never leaves you.

Makdiva: Yuck! What did u do today?

HotT: Nana took me to every living relative we have!

Makdiva: Huh? Why?

HotT: 2wish them Happy Holidays.

Makdiva: Christmas! All of our relatives are Christian.

HotT: Sorry! Anyway that took us from 8.00 after the 7.00 a.m., yes, A.M., mass till about 9.00 p.m.

Makdiva: UR Lying!

HotT: Nope! It's crazy! At least in England you can stay indoors with TV.

Makdiva: What's the TV like?

HotT: Completely different. Nana has satellite so it's

	cool. I mean, some of the programmes are a bit old, and flaming Lights Out doesn't help.
Makdiva:	What's Lights Out?
HotT:	Don't you remember? It's when the electricity gets cut. It's soo random!!
Makdiva:	Oh yeah.
HotT:	It's only for an hour or so mostly. Then generators come on, but only for the fridge and important stuff.
Makdiva:	OMG! I couldn't handle that. Nana has some dark corridors, plus those weird lizard-like things that crawl up the wall!
HotT:	I know! I found out that they totally hate loud noises. ☺

Tanisha and I absolutely hate creepy crawlies. When we were both little on holiday in Ghana, every two minutes we'd start screaming at anything that moved.

Makdiva: Guess what Nelson and I have

I could see she was typing.

HotT: NOOOOOOOOOOOOO! I don't want 2 know about u and Nelson cos that seems 2 get me punished!
Makdiva: OKAY! ☹

Mum walked in and sat on my bed, so I discreetly scrolled up past the Nelson bit.

'So how is she?' Mum asked.

'She's moaning about having to visit so many relatives on Christmas Day.'

'That's the best bit! Ask her how many presents she got.'

Makdiva: Mum's here. How many presents did you get?
HotT: Um . . . 15.
Makdiva: OMG!

Mum was laughing behind me. 'It's not so bad is it?' she said.

Makdiva: So whilst I was stuck here in the cold, making up the instant custard, u had present number 12 or something in your hands!
HotT: 14 actually. ☺ Don't mention custard – I bought the wrong brand and Nana was not impressed. Tell Auntie she said that the M&S pudding wasn't as good as last year.

I heard Mum tut-tut behind me. I could see her reflection in my PC and she had angrily folded her arms. It was funny when she and Nana-Amma got annoyed with each other. You could tell if there were no kids in the room there would be a major argument.

Makdiva: So unfair!
HotT: But I'm volunteering for a whole year. That's not going to be easy, u know my Twi is as bad as yours ☺, and then

<HotT logged off>
Makdiva: Tanisha??

'Mum, why has she logged off halfway through?' I asked.

'Looks like she got hit by Lights Out. You remember what that is, don't you?'

'Yeah,' I said. Then I began laughing. 'Just as she was justifying all those presents!'

'Yes!' Mum said, joining me. 'I think we should go there next Christmas or maybe the summer holidays – that's longer. You'd love it, Makeeda.'

'Yeah, maybe I would,' I said.

'You could visit the Manshia Palace and Museum'

'A museum?' I said. 'They're boring . . .'

'Makeeda, I'm talking about the King's home! Asantehene's palace?' Mum said, annoyed.

'Oh, so there would be stuff on Yaa Asantewaa?'

'Exactly.'

'Hmm . . .'

The more I thought about it, spending the holidays in Ghana didn't seem so bad after all. I mean, I knew I'd miss my TV programmes and friends, but they'd still be here when I got back. My eyes flicked to the white envelope addressed to Nelson on my dressing table. It contained a Christmas card and vouchers for his favourite music shop. I began to think about meeting him on the twenty-seventh. I was glad that we were finally going to talk things over, but part of me was scared. After all the misunderstandings, could we have a relationship left?

Chapter 18

Magic Moments

'Hurry up, Makeeda!' Dad shouted from behind my door. I'd just got out of the bathroom and couldn't find my tub of Astral body lotion anywhere. We were meant to be going to Aunt Anita's for dinner.

'Delphy! Where's my . . .?' I screamed.

'I haven't got it!' Delphy yelled back.

There was a knock on my door.

'I'm getting dressed!' I yelled back.

'Not without this,' Mum said, handing back my lotion. She was wrapped up in a dressing gown. 'Don't look at me like that – I ran out.'

Mum likes to bulk buy toiletries at half price. So we'll have loads of stuff for a while, then all of a sudden it will run out because she can't bring herself to buy it at full price. I have a sneaky suspicion that she's waiting for me to get a Saturday job at her favourite shop or something.

Within half an hour I was dressed in a top and blouse made of navy blue ntoma with yellow apples on it. Thankfully I had normal cuffs on this one. My yellow beads would have looked great with it, if I had known where they were.

When I got downstairs Aunt Grace was sitting on the sofa reading a magazine. She was wearing a long red dress with gold patterns on it. Her gold bangles jangled as she hugged me.

'This is a much better style than the last one!' said Aunt Grace, smiling. 'But you need a chain or something.'

'I know, but I couldn't find the one I wanted,' I replied.

'Makeeda, go and get your sister!' Dad interrupted.

'Delphy, hurry up!' I said, walking into her room.

She was watering her yam plant. Her hair had green ribbons in it that matched the colour of her ntoma.

'I'm coming,' she said. 'I just wanted to check on my plant.'

I stared at the plant. Despite the heat in the room, it still hadn't grown. I could feel my make-up melt and was about to force her out of the room, when I saw my yellow beaded necklace. The one I thought I'd lost. I marched up to her pink collection of hair accessories and pulled it out.

'Leave my pink — Oh,' Delphina began.

'What are you doing with my necklace? How many times have I told you not to go through my stuff?' I shouted.

'I . . . I . . . forgot,' Delphina said, scared.

I pushed past her and put the necklace on in her mirror. Delphina went back to staring at her plant.

'Delphy, it's not going to grow, you know,' I told her.

'It might!' she said defensively.

'Yams don't grow in —'

'La, la, la!' she sang loudly, shoving her fingers in her ears.

'Delphy!' I grabbed her arms, but she grew louder. 'Fine,' I said, just as Aunt Grace walked in.

'What's going on?'

'Makeeda was being mean to me and she said that my plant won't grow!' Delphy said, rushing into Aunt Grace's arms.

'Makeeda?' Aunt Grace said.

'And she pushed me,' Delphy added, crying.

'Apologise, Makeeda. There's no need for pushing.'

'But she stole my necklace,' I said.

'Do you have it now?'

'Yes, Auntie, but . . .' I began, but Aunt Grace gave me a severe look, so I apologised.

Delphy gave me a satisfied smile through her fake tears. It was all an act, as usual.

'Delphina, Makeeda's right,' Aunt Grace said.

'Told you,' I said, smirking, but Aunt Grace shot me another look, so I shut up.

'It's unlikely your plant will grow. We just don't have the climate for it here,' Aunt Grace added.

'But it's for my project. I can't go back to school without a plant. Everyone will laugh at me,' Delphy said.

'At least you tried. Now you get to write about why it didn't grow and stuff,' I said.

'Yes and it shows how mature you are,' Aunt Grace said looking straight at me.

I guessed that comment wasn't just meant for Delphy then.

'Besides, it's when things don't work out the way we expect, that the fun usually begins,' Aunt Grace said, smiling.

What was she talking about? There's no fun when things don't work out. Just grief! Delphy would probably fall for it though.

'Come on, let's go.' Aunt Grace said ushering us out.

An hour later, we had arrived at Auntie Anita's place.

'Ring the bell then,' Dad said to me.

The door opened to reveal a smiling Afua, so I knew straight off that I wasn't going to enjoy the party. I tapped my coat pocket for my mobile phone and felt relieved at its presence. After greeting everyone, I found my usual spot on the stairs and switched on my phone.

Bharti: W R U?
Bharti: Oh yeah, you're at that dinner thing. I think u need to talk to Mel about the whole Laura thing.

That didn't sound good. Actually it sounded like Bharti and Mel had been talking about me behind my back.

Mel: W R U? Can u call me ASAP?

Right, so Bharti the traitor has been telling Mel exactly what I think of Laura. Great!

I called Mel on Dad's phone. He always had loads of credit.

'Hi, Mel, it's me.'

'Hi, Makeeda. Are you out of credit again?'

'Yeah. What's the emergency?'

192

'You and Laura!' Mel said. 'Listen, I know you have issues with Laura but —'

'Mel, she doesn't like me, you don't always hear everything she says to me,' I said defensively.

'Bharti reckons that you don't like Laura because I'm hanging out with her more than you . . .'

'No!' I lied. I knew it would make me sound Delphy's age.

'Ohmigod, she's right isn't she?'

'No,' I lied again.

'Makeeda, I'm not being funny or anything, but you're not exactly into sports and stuff, are you?'

'Well no, not as much as you,' I replied.

That was an understatement. We were talking about the difference between watching an athletics programme on TV and going to the cinema.

'Yeah, well, Laura is. I'm not saying I have nothing in common with you any more but . . .'

I could see her point. It was easier to hang out with someone who was into the same things as you.

'It's OK, I get it,' I said, interrupting.

'Besides, I never said anything when you and Bharti started going off without me last year, did I?'

'No.'

It was always going to be awkward having three of us in a friendship, and Bharti and I did suddenly start spending more time together – especially when Mel got busier playing sports.

'Makeeda, you and I go way back pre-Bharti, pre-reception class!'

I started laughing.

'You know, if it wasn't for Laura, I wouldn't have known about what Nelson said to you. You know what I'm like when I'm on the phone.'

'Yes,' I replied.

I remembered a trip Mel took to Manchester a few years ago where she chatted to me through an earth tremor. It was only when her mother screamed at her to get off the phone and take cover that she realised what was going on.

'You should give Laura a chance,' she said.

'Hmm . . .'

Laura did me a favour in telling Mel what Nelson said that day, but she had still said some nasty things to me.

'Makeeda Amma Boakye, what do you think you're doing?' said Mum, angrily.

'Bye, Mel!' I said, quickly. 'Mum, I was just . . .'

'Get into that kitchen and help serve, like Afua. She doesn't have to be told,' Mum said, retrieving both phones from me.

I headed into the kitchen and was handed a tray of pies to serve to the other guests in the living room. Slowly moving around the room with a fake smile plastered to my face, I saw Afua engaged in a conversation with some adults.

'Makeeda,' Baby Akosua's dad said, beckoning me.

'Yes, Uncle Larry?'

He was dressed in a wine-coloured tie-dye shirt, and dark trousers. He automatically began speaking in Twi, until Afua interrupted him.

'Uncle, Makeeda, doesn't understand.'

'Oh yes, sorry. We were talking about the differences

between growing up in Britain and Ghana.'

'Ah huh,' I replied, trying not to sound bored.

'Your Auntie Anita reckons it's more difficult for children brought up here to get a firm grip of our culture, but I disagree. What do you think?'

'I, um . . .' Ohmigod, I don't care! As long as Mum gives back my phone, I'll do anything for my culture. 'Well, I guess it is.'

'Actually, I've been learning Adowa,' Afua said.

'Oh, that's very good Afua,' everyone chorused.

By this time we'd all sat down. My discarded tray of pies lay to my left, and I was using Aunt Grace's legs as a backrest, which she didn't seem to mind. It gave her an excuse to fiddle with my braids and generally make me look more ladylike.

'Yes, I go once a week after school,' Afua added.

I rolled my eyes and received a dig in the back from Aunt Grace. I was thinking of entering her for a psychic competition, when I saw my reflection in the mirrored fireplace and realised she could see everything I did.

'Makeeda, ever think of joining Afua?' asked Uncle Larry.

Not unless I was being paid to be in her company and, even then, I'd rather spend a week in three inch stilettos and a pencil skirt I couldn't walk in, I thought to myself.

'Um . . . not really, Uncle,' I said.

'Do you know what Adowa is?' Afua said, raising an eyebrow sceptically.

'Yes, of course she does, don't you, Makeeda?' Aunt Grace asked, making me turn to face her.

'Well . . .' I said, looking blank.

'Do you remember when you went to that dinner party?' Aunt Grace asked.

I must have returned a seriously dumb-looking face back, because when she continued I could hear the strain in her voice.

'The one at the hotel in Knightsbridge, when we had those children dressed in Kente . . .'

'Oh yeah!' I said, smiling broadly.

I could see the relief on her face. We may all have been family, but even Aunt Grace didn't want me to look stupid in front of everyone. Those children were really cute, especially the one who couldn't have been more than four years old. Ohmigod, I realised, Adowa is a dance!

'You know what? Maybe one day I'll join you on the dance floor, Afua, Ghana styleee?' I said, staring at Afua.

'Hey, then you two could give us a performance, couldn't you?' Uncle Larry said to Afua.

'Yes, Uncle,' she replied. I could see her face change from a frown to a smile at record speed.

'I'd better get this back to the kitchen,' I said, picking up the discarded tray of pies.

'Didn't they like it?' Auntie Anita said worriedly.

Behind her I could see my mother gesturing wildly for me to be as polite as I could. Auntie Anita is an OK cook, but sometimes she stresses for no real reason. Today she had good reason: there was no salt in the pies.

'Um . . . I think everyone's a bit, er . . . pied out, after Christmas,' I said, hoping that I might be able to escape.

'Oh right, take this then,' she said, handing a tray of mini sausage rolls.

'Okaaaaay,' I said, but Mum gave me a death stare. 'I'm sure these will be better, Auntie,' I added.

Then Mum threw her hands in the air in an 'I give up' way. That was when I realised what I'd just said. So I left quickly.

'Uncle Larry wants you,' Delphy said, grabbing a sausage roll as she ran past me.

'What?' I asked.

'She said Uncle Larry wants you,' repeated Kofi, as he too grabbed a sausage roll and raced past me.

I walked into the living room again but this time everyone just stared.

'Er . . .'

'Makeeda, is it true?' Aunt Grace asked.

'Um . . . what?'

'Delphina was probably mistaken,' Afua offered.

'Did you write about Yaa Asantewaa for a project?' Uncle Larry asked.

'Yes, for my history essay.'

Suddenly the tray of sausage rolls was taken away from me and all the adults were congratulating me.

'Such an achievement!' said one woman.

'Most children these days, they wouldn't be bothered,' said a man.

'I know,' Aunt Grace said, smiling at me.

I was really shocked at the attention. Usually I would just say hello to everyone and kind of disappear into that weird 'too old to be cute and too young to talk about politics' vortex.

Suddenly, I was the topic of conversation. I looked over at Afua; her arms were folded against her chest and she looked ready to kill me.

'So how did this come about?' asked an elderly auntie.

'Well, we had to do an essay about an historical woman we found inspirational. I chose Yaa Asantewaa,' I said.

'Oh, I see. Did you have to do the same?' she asked Afua.

Afua replied in Twi.

'Don't speak in Twi. Makeeda can't understand you,' the woman said.

'Sorry, Auntie,' Afua replied. 'I did mine on Rosa Parks.'

'Oh really? That was a good choice,' Uncle Larry commented.

'I agree, but why didn't you choose a Ghanaian heroine?' asked the elderly auntie.

'Oh, my school wouldn't let me,' Afua said.

I could see she was lying, but I didn't think highlighting that fact would score me any points. Ohmigod, I was being the better person. Yippee!

'My teacher didn't want me to write it because she thought I wouldn't find any books, but I just got stuff through the public library and online,' I said. 'She even tried to get me to change my topic but I wouldn't.'

'Did you get a good grade?' Uncle Larry asked.

'Yes, I got an A,' I said.

I knew I was being really smug, but I didn't care. Afua wasn't the only one interested in our culture.

'Oh, well done!' said the elderly auntie.

'Yes, it's very impressive,' said Uncle Larry.

'Thanks.'

'Yeah, well done, Makeeda,' Afua said, adding a fake smile.

'Well, your mum and I are very proud of you,' Dad said.

This came as a surprise to me. I turned around and saw a broad smile on his face and the same one on Aunt Grace's.

'Dinner's ready,' said Auntie Anita as she and Mum piled more food on to the dining table.

Afua pulled me aside. 'You know one essay doesn't exactly make you an expert, you know,' she said.

'Yeah, well, learning one dance routine doesn't make you one either,' I retorted.

'Makeeda, can you help me get some more drinks?' Aunt Grace asked.

'Um . . . OK,' I said, surprised. I could clearly see more than enough drinks already on the table.

'I heard that,' Aunt Grace said, once we were in the kitchen.

The smell of spicy rice wafted across us. Ohmigod, she's going to tell me off!

'I'm not going to tell you off, Makeeda.'

That's a relief. 'Thanks, Auntie.'

'I just want you to realise something. You and Afua aren't as different as you think.'

I clasped my mouth with my hand. It was the only way to stifle the threat of seriously loud laughter.

'Stop that!' Aunt Grace said, irritated.

'But . . .'

'You are both striving for the same thing,' Aunt Grace said.

I just gazed at Aunt Grace like she had just grown an extra head. There was no way Afua and I were alike, so why were we having this conversation?

'Whether you like it or not, she is your cousin.'

'Cousin? But how . . .' I said.

I always insisted on knowing how I was related to some-one. Once I asked my parents, they were forced to go through it step by step – something they didn't like doing, but it usu-ally resulted in the confirmation that the person was just a family friend.

'Her father's father and your grandfather, my father, were cousins.'

Mum walked in, and she and Aunt Grace spoke in Twi briefly.

'Wait a minute, father's father equals grandfather, plus your father equals cousins?' I said, unsure of myself.

'Yes.'

'So she's your niece too?'

'Well, yes,' Aunt Grace replied.

'Ohmigod!' I replied, shocked. 'It's OK not to like your cousin though, isn't it?' I said.

I suddenly realised that that question definitely should have stayed in my head. Mum shot me her death stare.

'Makeeda, her family are passing through some difficulties and it would help if . . .' Aunt Grace began.

'But she's mean to me,' I interrupted.

'You're mean to her,' Mum said.

'Well, I don't react well to being insulted,' I replied.

'Don't be so cheeky!' Mum said.

I saw Aunt Grace's features turn from a frown to a smile, then back again.

'Makeeda, just make an effort, for me?' Aunt Grace asked, before leaving me in the kitchen with Mum.

'OK,' I lied.

As we all sat eating dessert of ice cream and lemon cake, I overheard a conversation in Twi between an elderly man and the elderly woman from earlier. I looked over at Afua and I could see she too was eavesdropping, except I only understood the three words spoken in English as opposed to what sounded like hundreds spoken in Twi. I watched the expression on Afua's face change. She looked angry.

The elderly woman said my name and my ears pricked up.

'Can't they speak Twi?' the elderly man asked.

'No,' Aunt Grace replied. 'Afua, Makeeda, come here. Uncle Yaw wants to ask you something.'

I'd never seen the man before, so I knew he had to be some kind of family friend. Afua and I silently rose and sat near the elderly man.

'Uncle Yaw was just saying that since he's been here, he noticed that the children brought up in England don't seem to be interested in learning about their culture.'

'Huh?' Afua said.

I stared at her. I've never seen her give or make an incredulous sound like that before, to an adult anyway.

'Why?' I asked.

'Oh, I expect you prefer to keep in with your friends by not being seen as different,' he said.

'Huh?' Afua said again.

Even when the elderly woman told Uncle Yaw about Afua's dancing and my essay, he still didn't seem impressed.

He told us that there was nothing wrong in preferring our English culture to our Ghanaian one.

That's when I got upset. I told him that it wasn't a matter of preference, as we lived with both, but had more access to English culture than Ghanaian because we lived in England. I looked over at Mum and Dad. Mum was busy picking up the empty bowls, whilst Dad was pretending not to listen as he and Uncle Larry attempted to repair a broken remote control. I was waiting for them to stop me. They didn't.

Afua commented that it would help if our elders had sought to secure our interest by providing or organising more than Independence Day events for the next generation. Then I added if there were Twi language schools, like the ones people went to for Spanish, Portuguese, Arabic and Greek, then maybe by the time Ghanaian kids were adults they'd be fluent.

The room began buzzing in Twi, and Afua and I hadn't even noticed that we now had everyone's attention. Mum stood by the door, watching me, then smiled as she left the room.

Afua and I stared at each other and I looked away, embarrassed at our outburst. I could see Uncle Yaw looking impressed.

'I stand corrected. There are obviously two very bright and culturally literate young people around. I just hope that there are more of you.'

I surreptitiously looked at Afua. She had the same fire in her eyes as I had. I realised that she had something to prove. Even if I did too, it didn't mean Aunt Grace was right about us being similar, though.

'Girls, never forget the sacrifices of those who first came to England. It is because of their experiences that your generation have a lot more opportunities,' Aunt Grace remarked.

Sometimes I hate adults. They always have to be right.

I left the room and reclaimed my seat on the stairs. It was eight o'clock. I knew that this time tomorrow I would either be single again or still with Nelson. It wasn't going to be just another day hanging out with my boyfriend. That thought unnerved me.

Chapter 19

Crisis Talks

I felt nervous as the bus pulled into the garage. I knew that whatever happened today, Nelson and I would have to resolve everything, even if it meant us splitting up. He said that he hadn't called to dump me, but what if he just wanted to do it in person? I knew he was hurt that I hadn't been honest with him, but how could I?

My phone rang just as I jumped off the bus. It was Nick.

'Makeeda!'

'Yeah?'

'I just wanted a quick chat.'

'Now? Right at this moment?' I asked. 'Nick, I'm about to meet Nelson.'

'Yeah, I know.'

Ohmigod, was Mel right? Was Nick about to confess his

true feelings for me? I headed for a corner outside of the shopping centre's entrance, to get out of the way of the shoppers all eager for a bargain at the sales. This was going to be awkward. I didn't fancy Nick! I've never fancied him. How could I? It was Nick!

'Listen, I don't know how to say this, but I really don't fancy . . .' I began but stopped, realising I'd just spoken over him. 'What did you just say?'

'I just wanted to say I hope it works out for you two.'

'Oh, right,' I said, relieved.

'What did you say?'

'Can't remember,' I lied.

'Oh, I thought you were telling me you fancied something.'

'Nope, it's really noisy here. So what are you doing today?' I said, changing the subject.

'I'm going bowling with Anoushka.'

'Ohmigod, Anoushka as in Amazonian Anoushka?'

'Uh huh. I didn't even know she's Polish!' he said excitedly. 'I met her at my nan's. Apparently her grandparents and mine were old friends back in Warsaw.'

'Ohmigod, that's brilliant!'

'I know!' he said. 'I really owe you.'

'What for?'

'Well, you introduced us when she came to your house.'

'That was last year, Nick!'

Nick was at my house a couple of times when Anoushka was tutoring me. They got on, but there were no sparks or anything.

'I know, but she never forgot me! Anyway, I just wanted to

say . . . Nelson seems nice enough, but if he hurts you, I'll rip his . . .'

'It's OK, I get it,' I said, interrupting. 'If it's all right with you, I'm going to find out if I have a relationship left. Bye and say hi to Anoushka!'

'Definitely!' Nick said, and hung up.

I was glad he was finally being nice about Nelson, but even happier that he and Anoushka had got together. I was so glad that Mel had been wrong.

I turned my phone to silent and made my way through the people standing at the bus stop. Nelson was in the lobby dressed in black jeans and a black jacket. He hadn't seen me, so I quickly checked my reflection in a display window. My hair was tied away from my face and I had on a purple top and a pair of black trousers under my pink jacket and pink flats. I reapplied my lip-gloss. As I walked up to him, my nerves suddenly hit me and my mouth went dry.

'Makeeda, you made it,' he said, smiling. He tried to kiss me but I dodged him.

'Yeah,' I said.

I saw a look of disappointment in his eyes, but I didn't want to be a hypocrite and pretend that everything was fine.

'Shall we go to a coffee shop where we can talk?'

'OK,' I said.

It was weird, walking around with him. There were so many people that it would have been easier if we were holding hands. As it was, we got separated four times on our way to the Italian café. Every time he grabbed my hand, I shook him off.

'I didn't want to lose you again, that's all,' he said defensively.

'OK.' I shrugged.

'Makeeda, don't be like that.'

I ignored him and kept walking till we reached the café. I bought a drink and sat down at the corner table, overlooking the shoppers below. Nelson sat opposite me with a drink and a plate of chips.

'Sorry, I'm starving,' he said, tucking into his food. 'Want some?'

I sighed. 'No thanks.'

There was an awkward silence between us as I waited for him to finish eating. It just made the situation worse. I wanted everything to be over. I wanted to know whether he was really going to dump me.

'I'm glad you came,' he said.

'Right,' I said.

'I can't believe you thought I called to dump you,' he said, reaching for my hand. I moved back from the table.

'Makeeda? Can't I touch you any more?'

'Stop pretending, Nelson. I know why I'm here. You want to dump me in person.'

'How many times do I have to tell you? I don't want us to break up! I really like you!' he said.

I stared at him. None of this made any sense to me. Here he was telling me that he liked me, but all I could feel was anger towards him because of the way he treated me.

'Whatever!' I said. 'But that doesn't explain standing me up or the stuff you said in front of your mates.'

'Yeah, I know, Makeeda. I'm sorry, but you must believe me when I say I like you.'

'Why?' I asked.

'Why what?'

'Why do you like me?'

'Umm . . . I like the fact that you're totally obsessed with lip-gloss.'

'No, I'm not. What else?' I said.

'I like the fact that you are interested in your culture.'

'Huh?'

'I heard about that essay you wrote, against your teacher's advice. I was really impressed.'

'Thanks.'

'Why didn't you tell me about it?'

'I . . . I didn't think you'd be interested,' I said.

'Why not? You don't think that I'm only interested in music do you?'

'I . . .'

'Oh great! So you think that's all I'm about!' he said, irritated. 'Well, I guess we don't know each other that well.'

He had a point. I had no idea if Nelson had any other interests beyond music. I'd never asked.

'So, come on then – what else are you into?'

'Well, every weekend I go to South London and help out in a Portuguese school.'

I was shocked. I'd never asked Nelson why he couldn't see me on a Saturday. I suddenly felt guilty. Maybe I wasn't such a good girlfriend after all.

'Surprised?'

'Yeah. Why didn't you tell me?'

'Well, I didn't think you'd be interested.'

I guessed I deserved that. Once again silence enveloped us, and we stared at the shoppers laden down with red bargain bags. It wasn't going the way I thought it would. I thought we'd apologise, kiss and make up – with lots of kissing – or simply apologise and agree to be friends. Right now I was just confused. He angered me, but I still liked him. It was a weird feeling.

'Makeeda, why didn't you tell your parents about me?' Nelson asked.

'I couldn't. They wouldn't have let me see you.'

'You could've told me. I would've understood.'

'I didn't want to hurt your feelings. Besides, I thought you'd dump me if you found out how difficult it really was to see me.'

'I'm not like that!'

'Yeah? Is that why you stood me up? You knew I was still grounded!'

'I apologised for that, but I was angry. Mel was telling me stuff about you that I should've already known. You made me look stupid!'

'So you'd thought you'd get me back?' I asked.

'Don't try and turn this around. If you'd been honest with me from the start, none of this would've happened.'

I knew he was right, but I just couldn't seem to get past the fact that he'd hurt me.

'You're not the perfect boyfriend you know!' I told him.

'I never said I was, but at least I don't hide stuff.'

'I don't do that.'

'Really? Then why don't you trust me with your private

stuff? I'm your boyfriend, but you'd rather tell your mates what's going on in your life than me.'

'What? That's rubbish!'

'It's true!' he said angrily. 'Think about it, Makeeda. How come I told you about my mum, but you never once told me anything that really mattered to you? It's like you can't share or something!' he said.

I felt like he knew somehow about the stuff between Tanisha and Mum, even though I'd never told him. I suddenly got angry and I stood up.

'That's not true, Nelson!' I said, and I walked out of the café.

'Makeeda? Makeeda?' Nelson called after me.

I kept walking until I couldn't hear his voice any more.

I was wading through the crowds when someone caught my arm.

'Get lost!' I said, before turning to see Afua holding onto me. She looked shocked at my outburst.

'Hey, I just wanted to say hello,' she said, smiling uncertainly.

'Oh, Afua!' I said, embarrassed. 'I'm sorry; I thought you were someone else.'

We moved to the corridor leading to the toilets, as there were less people there.

'Are you OK?' she said, looking at me intently.

'Um, yeah,' I lied, wiping my face. I hadn't noticed I'd been crying.

Afua handed me a tissue and I just stared at it. Why was she being so kind?

'Don't worry, it's not used!' she said.

'Oh, I know. It's just that you and I aren't exactly . . .'

'Friendly? I'm sorry, I know I've been a bit of a . . .'

'A two-faced cow?' I offered.

'Um, yeah,' she said, looking embarrassed. 'Listen, yesterday made me think about stuff.'

'Hmm . . . me too,' I admitted.

'I thought making you look bad was the only way to get people to notice me,' Afua said.

'Right.' I didn't quite understand her, but I reckoned it had something to do with her parents, like most things did.

'Anyway, I was being out of order, so . . . I'm sorry.'

I stared at her. This had to be a joke: Afua apologising to me? I knew she was being genuine, because she actually looked nervous. The thing was, apart from stressing about meeting Nelson, at the back of my mind I knew something between Afua and me had shifted. Yesterday *had* changed the way I thought about her. She wasn't just showing off about her knowledge, she was proud of it, and in a funny way she had made me proud to be learning about our culture too.

'Well, I'm sorry too,' I said.

'What for?'

'For all the seriously mean names I've called you.'

'Er . . . when?'

'In my head,' I said.

'Oh,' she said, smiling. 'Do you reckon you'll ever stop doing that?'

'Dunno yet, but I can try,' I said, returning her smile.

A girl about our age, dressed in a department store uniform, waved to her.

'Listen, I have to go, but I'm glad I bumped into you,' she said, suddenly hugging me.

I was more than a bit shocked, as we never hug. In fact, we'd never even touched. Even when our mothers tried to make us hold hands for a photograph when we were five, we pulled apart.

'Yeah, me too,' I said, returning it and she left.

As I began walking, my phone rang. It was Bharti.

'Well, are you two sorted then?' she asked.

'Yeah,' I replied automatically, thinking that she meant Afua.

'So we can go shopping?'

'Shopping? No, not today. Nelson and I still haven't sorted everything out,' I said.

I told her about my argument with him but, when she suggested we meet up, I said no. I actually wanted to be alone. I needed to think; everything was whizzing around in my head. I knew Nelson was right about a lot of things. I should've told him about my parents, but I didn't think it was just about trust. I suddenly realised I was so used to keeping things in that it was actually difficult for me to be open with the right people.

I knew the real reason I'd walked out of the café was because I was scared. I was scared that he was right about me not being able to share my feelings, and I didn't like what it meant for all my relationships – with my friends, with Mum, with him. If I couldn't tell people how I felt, how could they ever truly understand me? I realised that bottling things up seemed to cause problems in all my relationships. It made me so aware of my feelings that I couldn't begin to consider how other people felt.

The more I thought about it, not being honest with everyone was a bit like lying to them. I didn't want to be that girl. But I knew that girl was me. What if I couldn't change?

I headed to HMV and began angrily flicking through some CDs. When a sales assistant approached me, I must have frightened him off, because he didn't even manage to get halfway through his polite enquiry before he abruptly left. I even saw the security guard giving me a cold stare.

I was having a weird day. Somehow I'd broken up with my boyfriend and made up with Afua.

A Fairytale track was being played. It reminded me of Nelson, so I began wading my way through the crowd towards the entrance. I got as far as the shop doors when my phone beeped with a text message.

Nelson: W R U?
Me: I'm outside HMV.
Nelson: Don't move!

Five minutes later I felt a tap on my shoulder. I turned to see Nelson.

'Makeeda,' he said. 'Why did you storm off like that?'

'I . . .' I began. This was my chance to tell him about Mum and Tanisha, but I couldn't. 'I'm sorry,' I said finally.

The words seemed to hang in the air. I started crying, because I thought that I was doing the same thing again – holding everything in. Except this time Nelson would surely dump me for it.

'I'm sorry I never told you about my parents. I didn't think it was an issue. I was wrong,' I said tearfully.

'It's OK, I understand,' he said, hugging me. 'I shouldn't have treated you like that, Makeeda. I was too angry to hear your side of it. I didn't think. I just wanted to hurt you,' he said.

'It's OK, I deserved it.'

We pulled apart and he looked me straight in the eye.

'I didn't mean what I said in the café. I know you trust me and, when you're ready, you'll tell me what's going on,' he said.

'Thanks,' I said, relieved. I was actually surprised. I thought it would be easier to tell him everything. I was wrong again. I guess it's something I have to work on.

'None of this changes how I feel about you, Makeeda,' he said, wiping my face.

'That's good to hear,' I said, smiling.

He hugged me again and I suddenly felt like I was floating. I knew I'd explain about Mum and Tanisha to him one day but, if he wasn't in a hurry, neither was I.

'Oh yeah, this is for you,' I said, handing him his present.

'Wow, thanks!' he said excitedly. 'Here you go,' he said, handing me a small, rectangular box covered in silver wrapping paper.

I opened it to find the latest MAC lip-gloss.

'Thank you!' I said. I was pleased and surprised.

'You know you're right,' said Nelson.

'About what?' I replied, applying my new lip-gloss.

'I am all about my music.'

'Yeah, I know,' I told him.

He used his envelope to hit me on my bum.

'Hey!' I said.

'Well, you can't deny your lip-gloss obsession!'

'Like I would!' I said, kissing him.

'Wow, Makeeda!' he said grinning. 'That was . . .' he began.

I had a feeling that, if anyone asked him again about his best kiss ever, I'd definitely get a mention.

Guide to Ghanaian Terms and Phrases

Ghanaian Terms

Adowa
A traditional dance, and also music, of the Akan people of Ghana.

Akan
Refers to the first group of settlers who came to modern day Ghana who form the largest ethnic group in Ghana. It consists of several politically independent units, such as the Asante, Akim, Akuapem and Kwahu.

Asante (Ashanti)
A region in Ghana. The Asantes constitute the largest single political group of the Akans and speak Asante-Twi.

Asante Kingdom
Created between the 16th and 18th Centuries and comprised of many states united under Osei Tutu the first Asantehene. It gained wealth through trade and conquests.

Asantehene
King of the Asante people

atwimɔ
Fried biscuits.

duku
Ghanaian style lady's head-scarf

durbar
An official reception held in colonial times between a local dignitary and a British governor.

Egweso (Ejisu)
A town close to Kumasi, the capital of Asante.

garden egg stew
A tomato-based stew made with egg-sized white or yellow aubergines

joloff rice
A traditional West African meal of fried rice with tomatoes, peppers, onions and meat.

Kente
A colourful Asante ceremonial cloth, worn at festivals, times of thanksgiving and special occasions. It is made of silk and woven on a hand-loom in strips, before being sewn together to form a larger cloth that is then made into garments.

Kumasi
Capital city of the Asante region in Ghana.

Manshia Palace
Asantehene's palace.

ntoma
African design usually made of cotton material.

outdooring
Public naming ceremony of a new born child.

plantain
Part of the banana family. Comes in two varieties: green (unripe), which are cooked like potatoes, and yellow (ripe), which are usually fried, roasted or boiled.

Twi
One of the main dialects of the Akan language, spoken by the Asante people.

Yaa Asantewaa
Queen Mother of the Egweso people who fought the British in 1900.

yam
A vegetable that grows in the form of tubers. It has rough brown skin (which is peeled before cooking) and a white fleshy centre. It is cooked in a similar way to potatoes.

Ghanaian Phrases

Akwaaba.
You are welcome.

Yɛ frɛ wo sɛn?
What is your name?

Yɛ frɛ me . ..
My name is…

I Tanisha ni?
Hello, is that Tanisha?

Wo ho te sɛn?'
How are you?

Me ho yɛ.
 I am fine.

Wo maame wo hen?
Where is your mother?

Kosɛ Nyame wɔ hɔ!
Accept my sympathies. God will help you to bear your loss.